Me, Myself and Ivy

Me, Myself and Ivy

Susan L. McElaney

This is a work of fiction. Names, characters, places, and incidents either are the products of the author's imagination or are used fictitiously, and any resemblance to actual persons, living or dead, business establishments, events, or locales is entirely coincidental.

ISBN: 1511884738
ISBN 13: 9781511884730

To my
beautiful
and
very special
granddaughter, Olivia.

I learn from you.
I am inspired by you.
And I love you more than you will ever know.

1

My name is Olivia, Olivia Breton—Livi for short. Until I was twelve, my life was pretty normal. I lived in Cape Cod, Massachusetts, in a small town called Sutcliffe, just one street away from the ocean in a little, shingled, three-bedroom cape with my mother, my father, and my sister, Ivy. Ivy was two years younger than me when she died—along with my mother and father—on July 10 in a freak car accident on the way home from Dairy Queen on a Saturday afternoon. I had gone to a sleepover party at my best friend Ruby's house the night before. I was returning home at ten minutes after two in the afternoon—exactly the same time that witnesses reported seeing my entire family wiped out on Route 28 by an eighteen-year-old drunk driver.

Somehow I managed to survive my excruciating loss. Even now, when I look back, it seems like one big blur in time—with no beginning, no middle, and no end—an enormous sadness, a massive emptiness, and an incredible feeling of hopelessness and despair.

But life *did* go on. I said good-bye to all my friends, including Ruby, and moved two hundred miles away to Chelsea, a small, quaint community in rural Connecticut. I would be living with Grammie and Papa—my mom's parents—in their massive, thirteen-room, two-hundred-year-old house. I had always loved visiting them with Mom, Dad, and Ivy, and I had always loved the occasional weekends that Ivy and I had spent with them during summer months. But in my wildest dreams, I never thought that I would move in with them permanently. However, as my dad used to say, "Never say never."

It was difficult—and scary—for me to leave all of my friends from Samuel de Champlain Middle School. I would have been starting seventh grade with them in just eight weeks, but that wasn't going to happen. I had to say good-bye to my old life: my family; my house; Mom's beautiful gardens; the purple bedroom I had shared with Ivy; the double-decker tree house Dad had built for Ivy and me; my private art tutor, Miss Karen; my school cross-country team, the Sutcliffe Striders; my dance instructor, Miss Evelyn; and my thinking rock which—hidden in the tall dune grasses that jutted up out of the white sands along the ocean—had, over the years, become my secret place to go to when I needed to be alone and explore my innermost feelings. I took my sweet apricot-colored poodle, Buffy, and we moved in with Grammie and Papa. I felt like I was walking under a monstrous, sad cloud. There was sadness all around me. Grammie and Papa walked with me under that same cloud. Even Buffy was sad. I was not used to *sad*. I didn't know how to live life feeling sad. I was only used to *happy*. I only knew, up until that time, how to live life feeling happy.

Grammie and Papa let me decide which of the bedrooms I would call my own. I chose the smallest and coziest room. It was at the top of the staircase that came up from the kitchen, a staircase no one ever used. Grammie said that one hundred years ago—fifty years before she and Papa had bought the house as a young married couple—my room was the caretaker's room, and he had used the private staircase so that he wouldn't disturb the family. He would let himself in through the kitchen and go promptly up the stairs and into his bedroom, which was tucked away at the far end of the hall away from the main grand staircase and the rooms that the family members occupied.

We spent one whole afternoon at Shetucket Hardware on the Green looking at paint samples. I finally decided that we would paint the walls of my room deep foam blue—like the ocean in Sutcliffe—and the window and ceiling trims would be painted the color of seashells. I had only been away from my old life for six weeks, but, besides desperately missing my family, I missed the ocean something fierce. From Chelsea, it was a thirty-minute drive to the ocean. At home in Sutcliffe, all I had to do was walk out the door, and I was on the beach in five minutes. Something I had always taken for granted had become a monumental void in my life. If ever I needed my thinking rock, it was now.

Grammie, Papa, and I worked feverishly to transform the long-abandoned room into something I would love, something I would feel safe in and look forward to coming *home* to. Papa wanted to buy me a new bedroom set, but I declined. I had already fallen in love with the antique white iron bed and the tall, bulky oak dresser that had a secret compartment hidden in the rear of the top drawer. Grammie and I went to Tillie's Fabrics in town and picked out white lace curtains to hang from the two large windows and a fluffy, white cotton down comforter for the bed. We found a sea-blue quilt to put at the foot of the bed and seashell-colored pillows to toss around the room.

Once all that was done, Grammie and Papa left me alone to unpack the personal items I had taken from my old life. Framed photos of Mom, Dad, and Ivy seemed to look at me sadly from the mantle over the fireplace. My favorite books lined the built-in shelves alongside the fireplace near my bed. Mom's favorite pale-blue flannel Snuggie—the one she wrapped herself in on cold winter evenings while we all watched TV together—rested on the arm of the worn oak rocking chair by one of the

windows. Dad's red-plaid flannel shirt with patched elbows—
the one he wore on Saturdays when he puttered in the garage
or worked in the yard—hung from the hook on the wall just
inside the door to my room. Ivy's purple heart-shaped pillow—
the one that she always clutched to her heart while we lay in
bed each night talking sleepily about things that sisters talk
about just before they drift off—rested on my own two pillows
at the head of my bed.

Ivy's portrait hung next to mine above the fireplace. Only
one year ago, Miss Karen had given us the assignment of painting a portrait of each other in watercolors. Little had we known
that they would soon be hanging together in my new room at
Grammie and Papa's house—*my* new house.

Back then, I had always become annoyed when people told
Ivy and me how much we looked like each other. "Oh my
God," they would say, "I thought you were twins!" I always
thought that was crazy because I was two years older than Ivy
and eight inches taller. But if I have to be honest, part of me
liked hearing what usually followed: how pretty our thick silvery blond hair was, how lovely it curled around our faces, and
how shiny and bouncy our long ponytails were. And I loved
hearing how beautiful our eyes were—how they shone pale
blue like forget-me-nots and how long and lush our golden
lashes were. Unlike most girls who had freckles, I actually
loved that both Ivy and I had a sprinkling of freckles across
our nose and cheeks.

My favorite uncle, Uncle Pete—my beloved godfather who
died from a heart attack when I was ten—always spoke of our
beauty and even wrote me a poem when I was in third grade
that I still had; it was tucked safely away in an old round hat box
that Grammie had given me when I was only about five years
old.

Here is to Livi, a sweet little girl.
Her hair is blond, her lashes curl.
I love you so, my little dove.
You'll always have my undying love.

And, just as Ivy and I had stared intently for hours at each other's face while we painted our watercolors—capturing every crease, every freckle, every dimple—it seemed that now our portraits stared eerily and sadly at each other; it was as though we had known back then, on some deep level, that one day our earthly connection would end, and we would connect only on a supernatural and spiritual level.

As the sun began to set at the end of that long day, I realized how weary I felt. I gently removed Dad's flannel shirt from the hook, picked up Ivy's purple pillow from my bed, and gathered up Mom's Snuggie and hugged them all tightly. I curled up in the big oak rocking chair and buried my face into my past, breathing in the familiar smells of my mom, dad, and sister. I needed to remember how they smelled. I was so afraid that I would forget.

I stared out the window at the massive old maple tree that seemed to engulf the house. I was up so high that I could have climbed out my window right onto one of the huge branches that twisted its way toward the sky. The white lace curtains fluttered in the cool evening breeze. I quietly watched as a fat robin perched on a distant branch, and I listened as she sang her beautiful melody. I imagined that we were in my old tree house—just Ivy and me—and I felt myself drifting off. I breathed in Mom, Dad, and Ivy.

I must remember how they smelled. I must never forget.

Then I heard Dad's voice, clearly and distinctly: "Never say never."

2

I woke up the next morning still curled up in my rocking chair. At some point during the night, someone had thrown my quilt over me. Buffy, still asleep, was curled up in a ball on my bed, snoring, twitching, and making muffled little barking sounds. Her legs moved as though she were running. I smiled, knowing that Buffy was obviously in the midst of a sweet dream—perhaps she was back at our old house, running with Ivy and me around Mom's gardens. I sighed, wishing I could have that same dream. No matter how I prayed for a dream about Mom, Dad and Ivy—and I did so each night before I fell asleep—I woke up the next morning realizing that I hadn't dreamed at all.

Again, I sighed. *Will this awful sadness ever go away?*

I climbed out of the rocking chair and moaned as the pins and needles in my legs slowly disappeared. *Oh, remind me to never sleep all night in the rocking chair again!* I limped over to my bed and plopped down next to Buffy. She awoke with a jump, but when she saw that it was me, she stretched and rolled onto her back so that I could scratch her belly.

"Mornin', Buffy-girl," I said sadly. That was all I had to say. Buffy knew exactly how I felt. Immediately, she rolled over and began licking my hand.

I love you, and I am here for you, her kisses told me.

I heard Grammie's footsteps coming up my private staircase. She tiptoed to my doorway.

"Oh, good! You're awake," she said as she came into my room and sat down on my bed. She stroked Buffy's belly. "Papa and I wondered if you wanted to come out to breakfast with us. Papa says it will do us all good—ya know, blow the stink off. We've all been cooped up in the house the past few days." Grammie looked around my room and smiled. She was pleased with the way my room had turned out. "Sweetie, I love your room. It's so cozy and warm. I hope you feel comfortable and safe here. I know this is so hard—for all of us—but I hope you know how much we love you and how wonderful it is to have you here with us. I wish it were under happier circumstances." She gulped back tears and waved her hand back and forth. "I'm so sorry, Livi. I didn't mean to do this."

I snuggled up to Grammie and lay my head on her lap. "Will this ever get better, Grammie?" I asked, letting my own tears spill out and run down my face.

"They say time heals all wounds," she said, letting her words hang in the air. She gently stroked my forehead with her fingers and tucked a long strand of my blond hair behind my ear. "We'll get through this together, sweetie—one day at a time, one hour at a time, if necessary. Papa and I are here for you, just as *you* are here for us." She leaned over and kissed my forehead. "Come on, Livi. Let's make Papa happy. Let's go and blow the stink off. I'm starving!"

Later that day, after we returned home, a soft rain began to fall, and it didn't look like it was going to let up.

"This rain is a blessing," Grammie said. "My gardens are in serious need of a good long drink, and Lord knows our well needs this too. Looks like a perfect afternoon to hunker down with a good book."

"I really don't feel like reading," I said. "And that's crazy, because I love to read. But I feel like doing something different for a change."

If I had been back in Sutcliffe, I would have been making plans with Ruby to go to the movies or maybe just walk on the beach. We loved to walk in the rain at the seashore. Mom would probably have said, "You're going to get wet!" And Ruby and I would have laughed.

I played the scene out in my head.

"Mom!" I'd say. "We live by the ocean! Of course we're going to get wet!"

"Good point," she'd say, laughing. "Well, just be home in time for dinner. I'm making a big pot of spaghetti and sausages. Ruby, you're welcome to join us."

"Thanks, Mrs. B!" Ruby would say as she dialed the phone to ask her mom. "Hi, Mom. Mrs. Breton asked me if I can stay for dinner tonight…Yup…Spaghetti and sausages…Yup…Okay, yup…I'll be home by eight…See ya…Love you, too."

"Woo-hoo!" I'd laugh. "Okay, let's go to the beach and get wet! Bye, Mom! Love you!"

The old wooden kitchen door would slam behind us, and I'd hear Mom say, "Love you, too! You girls be careful!"

Yes, I could just imagine it.

But, here I was instead, bored, sitting on a stool in Grammie's kitchen, drawing invisible tulips with my finger on the massive butcher block and trying to think of something to do—something different, something that would help get rid of the funk I felt, something that would ease the sadness I felt around my heart.

"I know!" Grammie said suddenly. "Do you feel like exploring?"

"What do you mean?" I asked, doubtful that Grammie's idea of exploring was the same as mine. "Explore *what*?"

"The attic!" she said excitedly. "That's always a fun thing to do. This old attic hasn't had anyone explore it since your mom was a little girl. She used to love to do that. She'd spend hours up in the attic going through all the old chests and crates. She always came down covered in dust and cobwebs but full of stories about her discoveries."

"Dust and cobwebs?" I asked. "Yuck!" But the more I thought about it, the more I liked the idea of spending time exploring the same attic that Mom had explored when she was a girl like me.

"Okay, Grammie! That sounds like a fun way to spend a rainy afternoon. I wonder if *I'll* discover anything interesting!"

3

The attic door stood opposite my own bedroom door in the up-stairs hallway. It squeaked loudly as I pulled it all the way open. I stepped up and onto the first step. I held the heavy door ajar behind me with one hand, afraid that if I let go it would slam shut, trapping me in the attic—like in some of the scenes in the spooky movies I had watched with Ruby. I curiously peeked up the winding staircase.

Eww, I thought. *This looks creepy.* Big cobwebs hung in the shadows from the huge beams above. Pieces of old horsehair plaster and other bits of debris littered the rickety wooden steps. I stepped up onto the next step and wrapped my hand around the handrail. It was loose and wiggled under my grasp.

"I don't know if this is such a good idea," I said out loud to myself. I slowly and gently released the door behind me and let it close. I held my breath as I tested the door to see if it would open again—it did. "Whew," I whispered. "Okay, here goes nothing."

I started my climb, one dusty step at a time, crunching the bits of plaster under my feet. I swatted frantically at cobwebs and invisible spiders, hairy insects, and anything else my mind was conjuring up. The handrail continued to jiggle under my tight grip. As I reached the top step, I breathed in the musty stagnant air. I heard the rain pelting the roof above me. The at-tic was lit only by the thin slants of light that filtered in through the two dusty windows—one at either end of the vast expanse. I swung my hand wildly overhead, searching for the pull cord that Grammie had said would light the one hanging bulb that dangled from the beam over the top step.

Where is *that darned thing?* It hit my hand twice as I randomly stabbed at the air overhead, and it continued to swing back and forth, just out of my reach.

Realizing that I was panicking foolishly, I forced myself to stop, take a deep breath, and calmly reach overhead for the cord. My eyes adjusted to the dim light, and I saw the long rope cord dangling above my head. I reached for the round wooden knob that was tied to the end. I gave it a quick tug, and suddenly a bright light bulb that hung in a silver lampshade flicked on and illuminated most of the attic.

"Okay," I said, exhaling loudly. "Now this is more like it! Time to explore!"

I stood frozen in that one spot and slowly scanned the entire attic. I wondered if my mom had been such a scaredy-cat the first time she had come up to explore. Had it been a dark, rainy day too? Had she felt the same relief wash over her when the overhead light had clicked on? Had she felt the same sense of irrational fear, mixed with the excitement of the hunt?

Are you here with me now, Mom?

I suddenly felt a calmness run through me. I felt warm inside, thinking that there was a chance that Mom was there with me at that very moment.

I miss you, Mommy. I really, really miss you. For just a fleeting second, I was sure I smelled Mom's smell—the same smell that I smelled on Mom's blue Snuggie that was thrown over the back of the rocking chair in my room below.

Where would Mom have looked first? My eyes were drawn to a dark area under the eaves. A big wooden chest was almost obscured from view. Several old and tattered silk gowns were heaped upon it as if someone had thrown them there in a big hurry. A pair of small gold slippers lay on the dusty floor near-by. A tall, dusty mirror stood on fancy legs and leaned against the side of the wooden chest. A metal clothing rack—from which several more dresses and gowns had been hung—stood behind the wooden chest and made a wall between the alcove and the rest of the attic. A few feet from the rack sat a red velvet chair with fancy armrests and spindly legs. Cobwebs and plaster debris covered the velvet seat cushion. A few feet away, a ladder-back chair faced an old mahogany desk. Papers were strewn across the top of the desk. I walked closer to the darkened area and realized that this corner had been intentionally walled off from the rest of the attic. It was someone's secret hideaway. I cautiously moved closer to the desk so that I could investigate the papers that lay scattered atop it. Hundreds of little tulips had been meticulously drawn on manila paper and painted beautifully in shades of red, white, pink, and yellow. Several paintbrushes stood upright in an old glass pickle jar, and a dozen small tubes of dried-up watercolor paints lay neatly in a dusty old shoebox. I inspected the lower corner of one of the papers to see what was written there in childlike handwriting.

The light was dim, so I had to squint. *E-l-i-z-a-b-e-t-h-A-n-n-B-r-a-d-s-h-a-w.*

I gasped. "*Mom!*" These were my mom's paintings. I had discovered Mom's secret childhood hideaway!

Suddenly, I was no longer fearful of the dark and dusty attic. With my bare hands, I swept the cushion of the red velvet chair, ridding it of all the cobwebs and plaster debris. I closed my eyes tightly, took a deep breath, and blew off all the remnants of crispy dead flies and wasps. For a few moments, a cloud of dust and plaster hung in the air.

When everything settled, I plopped down onto the chair and gripped the fancy wooden armrests. I looked around and quickly realized that Mom must have guided me to this, *her* secret place, which was forever going to be *my* secret place. It wasn't my thinking rock, but this would do. I sank into the soft red velvet cushion and curled up in my new thinking chair.

"Yup," I said out loud, "this will definitely do!"

No one else will be allowed up here, I thought. *Just me, myself, and I.*

4

The rest of the summer flew by. I spent part of every afternoon up in the attic. It was my secret place—except that I just *had* to tell Grammie all about it. She confirmed that my mom had originally assembled the hideaway back when she was twelve years old—exactly my age. Grammie assured me that no one else would need to know about it. It would be our secret.

"No one will be allowed in my hideaway," I said to Grammie, stretching to my tallest height and standing with my hands on my hips. "Just me, myself, and I."

That's what I always used to say when I wanted to be alone, when I didn't want Ivy to bug me: when I tried to curl up with a good book on the hammock in the backyard and Ivy decided she wanted to curl up on the hammock too; when I tried to go walking along the beach alone and Ivy decided she wanted to walk along the beach with me; or when I was upset about something and wanted to sneak away to my thinking rock to be alone and Ivy would show up and ask what was wrong.

"*Nothing! I just want to be alone! Can't I ever be alone?*" My words would echo against the rocks and continue along the shore. "Geez, Ivy, I just want to be *alone*—just me, myself, and I!"

Just me, myself, and I. What I wouldn't give now to have Ivy bug me. Being alone didn't feel so good. I missed Mom and Dad something awful. And I missed Ivy *really, really* bad. I was

definitely alone now—just me, myself, and I. And there was
nothing I could do to change that.

It took me several days to clean the Hideaway (that's what I
decided to call it) and to reorganize the space. I decided I needed to make the whole area bigger. I moved the wooden chest
to the side, placed the red velvet chair across from it, and slid
back the clothing rack—now heavy with the gowns and dresses
that had been piled on the wooden chest for the past quarter of
a century. With Windex and an old rag, I wiped away years of
dust and dirt from the tall mirror and its fancy legs, and then
I strategically leaned it against the eaves. Even though there
were no windows under the eaves, the mirror caught the light
from the windows at either end of the attic and brightened up
the Hideaway. Near the bottom of the mirror, a small crack
zigzagged across the glass and collected the light beams, sending fragments of rainbows throughout the attic. I discovered
a large braided rug rolled up in the corner behind the stairs
and dragged it into the middle of the big open floor area of my
"room." I unrolled it, and suddenly, my Hideaway was transformed into a den, a cozy parlor from a hundred years ago.

I made a big collage using some of Mom's tulip paintings,
and I hung it from the eaves above the big wooden chest. I
found several other paintings that Mom had done and hung
them from the eaves and among the remaining tulips. There
were images of gardens, cats, and snowmen. One painting fea-
tured a pretty red-haired girl with freckles. Mom had titled it
My Best Friend, Angeline.

I lovingly organized the art materials into my own art stu-
dio. I hadn't painted in months, so it was pleasing to me to be
able to spend time caressing my familiar wooden easel, special brushes, and tubes of paints. Grammie had found a long
wooden table hiding in the recesses of the attic, and she helped
me drag it into the Hideaway. Together, we situated it so that it

made the final wall of my secret room. I arranged all my paint supplies at one end. At the other end, piles of my art books found a home alongside folders filled with photos that I had collected over the years and pictures that I had ripped out of magazines. My plan had been to paint them one day. Well, *one day* had arrived. For the first time since Mom, Dad, and Ivy had died, I felt alive, content, and satisfied—no longer wishing that I had died with them. I still wondered what the reason was that I had been allowed to live, to go on without them. One thing was clear to me though: there *was* a reason. I just didn't know what it was yet.

Buffy and I spent the rest of that summer settling into our new home with Grammie and Papa. We were all getting used to a new way of life. Before I knew it, it was time to start seventh grade in my new school.

Grammie sat quietly in my rocking chair and watched as I carefully selected what I was going to wear the next day, my first day at Chelsea Middle School. Buffy was curled up on the foot of my bed on Mom's Snuggie, keeping one eye on me as I laid each piece of my outfit across my bed. I knew Grammie was nervous for me, so I tried to feel excited—like I would have felt if I were about to start seventh grade in my old school with all my familiar friends—but all I felt was a big sense of dread and fear.

How could I feel excited when I was going to a strange school where I knew no one and where no one knew me? How could I get on the school bus the next morning and face a bunch of total strangers? How would I find my way around my new school? Would anyone talk to me? Would I be able to make new friends?

Oh, Ruby! I miss you so much! Why can't things be like they used to be? Ivy, what I would give to have you here with me now, bugging me about what I should wear tomorrow. Instead, I am here all alone—just me, myself, and I.

I didn't realize that Grammie had gotten up from the rocking chair until I felt her hug me from behind. "I know how hard this is for you, Livi," she said softly. "You are starting a new life at a whole new school, missing Ruby and all your friends from home, and not knowing how everything will turn out. I wish there was something I could do to make all of this easier for you."

That was all I needed. I turned around and rested my head against Grammie's chest and sobbed. Grammie held me tightly and rocked backed and forth. A million different feelings passed through my mind and my heart. Nothing made sense to me—and yet, everything made sense to me. I knew what I had to do. I had to begin again.

"I'm okay, Gram." I sniffed as I wiped my eyes with my sleeve. "I can do this. I know I can do this."

5

I stood alone at the end of my driveway. Before I could see the big yellow bus, I heard the roar of its engine as it turned the corner and headed up Cider Mill Road. I picked up my backpack and hoisted it over my back and onto my shoulders. I said a silent prayer to Mom, Dad and Ivy.

Please help me to have a good day. Please help me to just remember to be myself. Please stay with me.

The bus rumbled to a stop. With a loud blast of air, the doors opened. I heard the sounds of kids laughing and talking. I took a deep breath, held my head up, and carefully climbed the three stairs that led to the rest of my life.

Although I was panicking inside, I forced myself to appear calm; I scanned the bus but saw no empty seats. It suddenly became quiet as I walked down the aisle toward the back of the bus. I was aware that everyone was looking at me and that some kids were whispering, but my heart was pounding so hard and loud that I couldn't hear what they were saying. Out of the corner of my eye, I saw someone stand up near the back of the bus.

"There's an empty seat back here," a pretty brunette shouted to me. She had needed to stand to be heard, and she sat back in the seat and slid toward the window to make room for me.

"Thanks," I said to her as I removed my backpack, set it on the floor, and plopped down next to her. I smiled and said, "Hi! I'm Livi."

"Hi, Livi. I'm Brooke." Her sandy brown hair was thick and borderline frizzy. A ponytail—secured by a red scrunchie—fell just to the nape of her neck and bobbed in time with the bouncing of the bus. Her chocolate-brown eyes had specks of gold that reflected the sunlight streaming in through the window next to her. "You're new here; where are you from?" she asked.

"I just moved here from Sutcliffe, Massachusetts," I said, relieved to be in a conversation and out of the spotlight of everyone on the bus. "What grade are you in?"

"Seventh," Brooke said. "You?"

"Me too," I answered. I smiled in response to Brooke's big smile. Just like me, she had a mouth full of silver braces. I looked into her dark brown eyes and suddenly felt more comfortable. In my head, I heard a voice: *Go for it. Just tell her the truth.*

"I gotta tell you, I am *really* nervous. It is kind of scary starting at a new school and not knowing anybody." *There! I said it.* "Thank you so much for rescuing me when I first got on the bus."

"Oh, you're welcome. The truth is, I know exactly what you are going through. I just moved here a few years ago, so I know how scary it is." Brooke patted me on the hand. "I'll help you find your way around. Do you know what homeroom you're in?"

"I really don't know anything. They told me to report to the office before I start my first class today—and I don't even know where *that* is." I sensed curious eyes watching me. I tried to smile in their direction, but as soon as I did, they quickly looked away. "This school has so many buildings; it looks more like a college than a middle school. Back home, our middle school has only one big building." I smiled at Brooke and sighed. "I'm worried that I won't be able to find any of my classes."

"No worries. I'll show you where to go. Maybe I can walk you to your homeroom. What is your last name, Livi?" Brooke asked. She was leaning forward, struggling to adjust the strap on her backpack.

"Breton," I told her. "What's yours, Brooke?" My breathing had started to slow down.

"Brennan," Brooke said. She gave up on the strap and tossed the backpack to the floor. "Hey!" she said, sitting up straight in her seat. "We must be in the same homeroom! They go alphabetically: Brennan, then Breton! Oh, how cool is that?!"

Two girls seated a few rows up from us turned and called out to Brooke. "What's all the noise back there?" said the girl closest to the aisle. They both laughed. "Who's your new friend?"

"This is Livi. She's in seventh grade with us!" Brooke said as she stood and leaned over the seat in front of us. "Livi, this is Manda. She's the smart one—pretty crazy but very smart."

Manda's laugh was deep. Her chestnut-brown hair hung just below her shoulders, straight and shiny, and was tucked loosely behind her ears. Her eyes—as chestnut brown and shiny as her hair—disappeared under thick, brown eyelashes when she laughed.

"Yeah, I am pretty smart, and I guess I'd have to say I am pretty crazy too!" Manda said. She had a surprisingly deep voice. "Welcome to Chelsea Middle School, Livi!"

"And this is Lilly," Brooke said, pointing to a thin, frail-looking, red-haired girl. "She is the quiet one, but if you ever need an answer to a trivia question, she is our whiz kid."

Lilly's pale skin began to blush. Her red hair—almost the color of cinnamon—was full, long, and wavy, and her bangs just touched her pale, cinnamon-red eyebrows. I was struck by her large, almost angelic, pale blue eyes that had a sort of sadness about them. She flashed me a shy smile before she lowered her head; all I could see were her full and long pale eyelashes that seemed to be resting on her cheeks as she looked down at the floor.

The rest of the ride to school was uneventful. I felt pretty comfortable. I didn't say too much, but I smiled a lot; I was amazed how much these girls reminded me of my friends back home. Some of the other kids around us started to join in the conversation.

This might be okay. This might just be okay. When I looked over at Brooke, she was smiling at me, so I smiled back at her. *Thank you, Brooke.* I took a deep breath and let it out. *Yup, this might just be okay.*

6

I just don't get *this math!* I threw my pencil across my room. *What is* wrong *with me? I* never *have trouble with math!*

"Okay, I am going to read this one more time, and that's it!" I said. But instead of looking at the story problems, I looked out my window, mesmerized by the beautiful colored leaves. It seemed that just yesterday they were all still a vibrant green. I was amazed how Mother Nature always seemed to know the exact moment for autumn to begin.

It was only six o'clock at night, and already the sun had begun to set. The front of our house faced the southwest. Grammie said that back in 1790, when our house was built, people always oriented their houses with the front of the house facing the southwestern sky, so people could sit on their front porches and admire the sunset. My bedroom window faced the sunset, and this evening it was putting on quite a show. The sun was a bright red fireball, and the sky around it was bathed in various shades of red. *Red sky at night, sailors delight; red sky in morning, sailors take warning.* That's what Mom always used to say. And her prediction was always right. *Guess it's going to be a nice day tomorrow.*

I redirected my eyes to my worksheet.

Justin is making snowballs to build a fort on the winter break. Justin can build 15 snowballs in an hour, but 2 snowballs melt every fifteen minutes. How long will it take him to build 210 snowballs?

It was hard to believe that I had already been in my new school for two weeks. Last week, it had still felt like summer, but over the past few days, there had been a chill in the air while I waited for the bus in the early morning. This evening, the cool breeze gently ruffled the lace curtains at my windows. I had goose bumps, so I pulled up the quilt from the foot of my bed. Buffy jumped up onto my bed, landing square on my math worksheet. The paper ripped, but I didn't care. I rolled over and snuggled up next to her; tears came out of nowhere. I felt sad, but the tears felt good. I didn't have to explain anything to Buffy. She just always knew what I was feeling deep inside. She licked my cheek and made me smile. I was smiling and crying all at once. I thought I was going crazy.

I reached for the diary that Grammie had given me earlier in the day. Its cover was quilted and decorated with red, pink, and yellow tulips. I untied the red ribbon and opened it. Grammie said she had found it earlier that day in her vanity drawer.

"I forgot I even had it," she had said. "I always wanted to keep a daily journal—you know, to write my feelings down at the end of each day—but I never got around to it. I thought maybe you'd like it. It is just too pretty to sit in a drawer and go unused."

In my literature class that day, Mrs. Kneeland had introduced us to an autobiography called *The Diary of Anne Frank*, and I was intrigued with the whole idea of keeping a diary. Anne had felt scared and alone as she hid in an attic that kept her and her family safe from Hitler's army. She had decided to make her diary a personal record of letters to "Kitty"—a friend she had invented. And now, Grammie had given me my very own diary. I couldn't help but wonder if that was just a coincidence or if it was something much more. But what? Something spooky? I shivered as I thought of the possibilities. Was someone trying to tell me that keeping a diary might be a good thing? Was it supposed to be a healthy and meaningful way for me to make some sense of my confusion and my sadness as I floundered and struggled through this dark time in my life?

I breathed in a familiar smell—Jontue, Mom's perfume. For as far back as I could remember, Mom had worn Jontue, and apparently it was Grammie's favorite too. Until then, I hadn't realized how much I had missed it.

Funny, but I don't ever remember Grammie smelling like Jontue. But the journal was in Grammie's vanity drawer all these years, so it must have taken on the smell of Grammie's perfume.

I stuck my nose right into the journal and inhaled deeply. I began crying again. Again, I felt happy and sad all at the same time.

I reached for a pen and turned to the first page. Like Anne Frank, I decided to write "letters" to someone so that my writings would feel personal—connected. I began.

Monday, September 15
Dear Ivy,

    I am feeling very strange. I feel like my life is not my own. I don't know who I am anymore. I feel so alone and so confused. And I don't know what to do.

Love,
Livi

I closed the journal and tied the red ribbon into a small bow. Sighing, I rolled off the bed. I looked around and tried to find a place to put my diary—a secret place so that no one would ever see my private, deepest thoughts. Then I remembered the secret compartment in the rear of the top drawer of my dresser.

Perfect! No one will ever find my diary in there. I opened my top drawer and pushed my socks aside. Reaching my hand way into the back of the drawer, I slid the wooden panel to the right, placed my journal into the small cubby hole, and then slid the panel back to the left. To anyone else, it looked like the panel was just the back of the drawer. I pushed my socks back in place. Satisfied that no one would ever discover my secret compartment, I closed the drawer.

I plopped back down onto my bed and, once again, attempted to solve the stupid math word problem. Next thing I knew, Grammie was waking me up for school.

Oh, crap! I didn't even remember falling asleep. I hadn't finished my math homework. I hadn't gotten my clothes ready for school either. Rushing, I barely had time to shower, dress, and eat. The school bus would arrive soon.

I groaned. *This ought to be a wonderful day. I can just feel it in my bones.*

7

"Is there anyone who doesn't understand how to solve this math word problem?" Mr. Tauro asked.

I cringed. I was too embarrassed to raise my hand. I never—*never!*—had trouble understanding math. I had always been a whiz. I gasped inside when I heard Mr. Tauro call my name.

"Livi, would you tell us how you arrived at your answer?" I looked up to be sure he was talking to me. He was casually sitting on the corner of his desk. His blue polo shirt emphasized the deep blue of his eyes. He smiled at me and waited for my answer.

Oh, crap.

"Well, actually," I said, "I…I don't understand how to do this. I don't…I don't know why I just can't seem to get it. I've always loved math…but…I just can't seem to get *this*." I fought to hold back the tears, sensing all eyes on me. I heard a few snickers from kids at the back of the class. I thought I was about to die.

From across the room, I heard my savior—again: "Ugh. I know just what you mean, Livi. I was having the same trouble until all of a sudden—*bingo*—I *got* it. I think I was just over-thinking it." As Brooke shared her own plight with the entire class, I started to relax. I saw several others in the class nodding in agreement. I was not the only one who didn't get it. Brooke explained how she had learned to transform each word problem into a story that was more pertinent to her own situation, and she said that helped her work through the problem.

Thankfully, the bell rang, and class was over. "We'll talk more about this tomorrow," Mr. Tauro said, over the noise. "Do the best you can with tonight's assignment. Don't make yourself crazy! We'll figure it out together tomorrow."

I loaded up my backpack, slung it over my shoulder, and headed for the door.

"Hey, Livi! Wait up!" Brooke said from her desk two rows over. We walked out into the wide hallway. It was crowded with kids walking in both directions. We wove in and out of the chaos. "I wanted to ask you if you'd like to come to my house for a sleepover on Saturday. Manda and Lilly are coming, and I thought it would be fun for you to join us."

"Oh, wow—" I started, but felt at a loss for words. This was so unexpected. On one hand, I felt flattered and excited, but on the other hand, I felt petrified that I wouldn't fit in. These were not my friends from home—friends who I had had sleepovers with a zillion times, who I had felt so comfortable with, who let me just be myself. Brooke was not Ruby. With Ruby, I could be silly or serious. I could be talkative or quiet. I could be whatever I wanted to be. Ruby just always *got* me. I didn't have to worry that I would say or do the wrong thing. But if I decided to go to Brooke's sleepover with Manda and Lilly, I would feel like I was on display—like they would be looking at every little thing I did. I would be the outsider, trying to break into their little circle. And they might not like me. What if they didn't like me? I began to tremble. I knew Brooke was waiting for an answer.

"Sure. I just need to ask Gram. Thanks," I said, trying to sound enthusiastic.

We walked out to the bus together, and along the way, Lilly and then Manda joined us. Their chatter was directed toward Brooke and each other. I forced a smile and tried to feel included in the conversation, but I didn't even know what they were talking about.

Manda mentioned the sleepover to Brooke. "I can bring some popcorn Saturday night."

Brooke casually informed both girls that I would be coming too. Manda and Lilly quickly glanced at each other; for a split second, I sensed that they were surprised and maybe even a little put-out that I would be joining them. They recovered quickly.

"Oh, great! That is so cool, Livi. Hope you are not planning on getting much sleep," Manda smiled. Her dark eyes met mine.

"Yeah, cool, Livi," Lilly said. "I hope you have some neat ghost stories to tell us."

On the ride home, the bus was filled with the normal chatter. I found myself staring out of the window. I felt so out of place. I looked around. Everyone seemed so happy and *normal*. I felt a lot of things, but happy and normal were not among them. And right then, all I felt was *out of place*.

I was quiet at dinner, and I could tell that Grammie and Papa were trying to get me into a conversation.

"How was school today, Livi?" Gram asked as she spooned more mashed potatoes onto Papa's plate. I told her it was okay.

"Do you have much homework?" Papa asked.

"Nah," I said, "I already finished it—all but my math." I felt bad for Grammie and Papa. I knew they wanted me to assure them that everything was good: that I was liking school, that I was making lots of new friends, and that I was becoming happy again. I didn't have the heart to tell them that my life stunk: that I hated school, that I couldn't seem to find the energy to make new friends, and that I just wanted my old life back. I couldn't even look at them. I felt tears welling up in my eyes. I tried to hold them back.

And then the phone rang.

Grammie got up from the table. "Hello? Livi? Sure, just a minute." She handed me the phone. I was startled. This was the first phone call I had received since moving in with Grammie and Papa. With my eyes, I asked if it was okay for me to take the phone into the den. I noticed the relief in my grandparents' eyes. I saw them look at each other. And I saw their moods lift.

It was Brooke. She asked if I had talked to my grandparents yet about the sleepover. I told her no but asked her to hold on. I went out into the kitchen, holding the phone tightly to my chest so that Brooke couldn't hear me.

Grammie and Papa stopped eating when I told them about Brooke's invitation. They listened. Grammie asked me quietly if I wanted to go. I shrugged my shoulders and said, "I *think* so."

Grammie smiled her sweet smile and said, "Livi, I think that sounds like fun. If you want to go, it's okay with us." She looked across the table at Papa, and he nodded in agreement.

Brooke squealed with excitement when I told her I could go. I plopped down on the big, comfy chair in the den, and we talked about the party—what I should expect to do at the sleepover, what we would eat, what we should wear, and what movie we should watch. Brooke said I should bring nail polish if I had some cool colors, because we could give each other manicures and pedicures.

Then we worked through the math problem together, and, thanks to Brooke—*bingo*—I *got* it! An hour later, we reluctantly said good-bye. I told her that I had to go and finish my math homework now that I understood how to do those stupid word problems.

I told Grammie and Papa that I was going to my room. "I am tired, so I'll say good-night now," I said.

Then I ran up the stairs, taking two steps at a time. I dove onto my bed, waking Buffy from her nap. I curled up next to her and covered us both with my quilt. I was smiling, and I think Buffy was too. I was too tired to get into my PJs right then, but I was too excited to just lie on my bed, and I didn't feel like doing my math homework yet either. I sprung from my bed, opened the top drawer of my dresser, and reached toward the back. I pulled my diary from its secret place. Then I bounced back onto my bed, again waking Buffy who had just fallen back to sleep.

"Oops. Sorry, girl," I told her. I pet her head for a moment, and she quickly closed her eyes. I untied the red bow, opened my journal, and began to write:

Tuesday, September 16

Dear Ivy,

Well, this was an awful day! I couldn't believe that Mr. Tauro called on me to give him the answer to the math word problem! I hadn't even done my homework last night because I just couldn't understand it. I was so humiliated. But Brooke rescued me. Thank you, Brooke! I don't know if she knows she rescued me. She just is so nice and thoughtful, and she seems to know when I feel like I just can't go on. Anyway, Brooke invited me to her sleepover this Saturday—with Manda and Lilly. I've been trying to think of a way to get out of it, because I really am just too nervous to go. I don't feel comfortable going to this thing with girls who I hardly know. I miss Ruby and all my friends from home. I know Ruby would tell me to go. And, Ivy, I know you would tell me to go too. I can hear you both: "Livi, how are you going to meet new people and make new friends if you don't go? You have to get out of your comfort zone, Livi!" Ruby was always so wise. And, Ivy, although I never told you, you were much too wise for your young age. I know you would both be right. I am trying—I really am!

Well, guess what? Brooke called me this evening! It was weird getting a phone call. But it also felt so cool! We talked for over an hour, and it was just like when Ruby and I would talk on the phone until Mom or Ruby's mom would give us the "look" that meant we had to hang up. I think Brooke really likes me, and that feels really good. I hope that I get to know Manda and Lilly much better at the sleepover. I hope they like me. And I hope I like them too. I know I already like Brooke—my rescuer.

So, today started out being a bad day. I was really feeling like my life would never get better. But then Brooke called me. And I feel great now! And it feels like Brooke and I have always known each other. Thank God for Brooke!

Talk to you soon!

Love,
Livi

Finished, I hid my diary. Within ten minutes, I had completed my math homework. Piece of cake! I got into my PJs and climbed into bed, and, somewhere in the middle of my mental list of things to bring to the sleepover, I fell asleep.

8

Before I knew it, it was Saturday. I was so nervous about the sleepover. Gram was going to drive me over to Brooke's house at four o'clock. By three o'clock my backpack was loaded with everything I thought I might need, and my sleeping bag was rolled up and ready to go. I was wearing my aqua sweatpants and my matching MUDD zippered hoodie. I had pulled my long, wavy, blond hair back into a ponytail and wrapped it with an aqua scrunchie. Even though I was not allowed to wear make-up, I had brushed just a hint of sparkly blush on my cheeks and eyelids. I looked into the full-length mirror that was on the back of my bedroom door, and I gave myself the once-over.

I thought that I looked pretty, but I was worried that if I didn't resume cross-country running soon, my muscles would get flabby and weak. I made a mental note to ask Brooke, Manda, and Lilly if they knew anything about the cross-country team at school. Tonight I planned to tell them a little bit about my experiences running at Champlain Middle School last year.

Gram yelled up the stairs, "Livi, it's four o'clock—time to go." I gave Buffy a kiss and a scratch behind her ears, grabbed my backpack and my sleeping bag, and ran down the stairs to the kitchen. I gave Papa a kiss on the cheek.

"Have a nice time, Liv," he said. "See you tomorrow!"

At the door, I looked back at Papa. "Love you, Papa," I said, and I smiled.

"Love you too, Liv. Just be yourself. You will be fine." I gave him a thumbs-up and left.

Gram and I turned right onto Hickory Street. Brooke lived at number 66. We drove slowly down the treelined lane. The houses were big and sprawling, and the yards were spacious. A few boys were skateboarding down the slate sidewalk that lined the road. At the same moment, Grammie and I spotted number 66.

"There it is—sixty-six," Grammie said first.

Together we said, "Wow! What a house!"

A large stone house with a maroon double door sat among a variety of plush bushes and shrubs. Several grand oak and maple trees adorned the beautifully manicured lawn. A winding stone path led to the front porch. I said good-bye to Gram, slammed the car door, and hoisted my backpack over one shoulder and my sleeping bag over the other. I watched Gram drive away. I walked along the winding path and made my way up the two stairs to the porch.

I jumped when, from the far end of the porch, I heard Brooke say, "Hey! I'm over here!" She was sitting on a white wicker chair with her legs curled up under her. "You're the first one here. Manda and Lilly should be here any minute."

I walked toward Brooke, set my stuff down, and leaned against the porch railing. Grapevines ran along an arbor and provided shade and privacy to the far end of the porch.

"Wow, this is really cool," I said as I admired Brooke's sheltered area.

"Yeah," Brooke said, giggling. "I call it my 'hideout.' I can sit out here in broad daylight, and no one even knows I'm here. It's my go-to spot when I want to be alone."

I smiled and wondered why I didn't tell Brooke about my own hideaway.

Maybe someday—but not today.

From a distance, we heard girls giggling. We secretly watched as Manda and Lilly trudged up the sidewalk, laughing and obviously absorbed in a private joke.

"Let's spook them!" Brooke whispered. "When I give you the sign, we'll yell *Boo!*" We squatted down in the dark recesses of the long porch. I felt foolish; I hardly knew Manda and Lilly. If I were at home with Ruby and my other friends, I would have loved it. But right then, I felt dumb.

Still giggling, the girls climbed the steps onto the porch. Brooke put one finger up in the air and then whispered, "Now!"

But only I popped up—and only I yelled "*Boo!*"

Both girls screamed and ran back down the steps.

"*Aaaah,*" Manda moaned.

Lilly was hanging onto Manda's arm. "Geez!" she said. "Give me a heart attack, why don't ya?"

I was horrified and confused, and I looked at Brooke. "I thought *we* were going to spook them—*together.* What happened?"

"Well, that is just a *weird* thing to do," Brooke said. She rolled her eyes as she looked at Manda and Lilly. "C'mon, let's go inside."

Am I missing something? The only thing weird *here is the fact that it was Brooke's idea to do this dumb prank. And now she is acting like it was* my *idea. I don't get it.* I saw Manda and Lilly exchange annoyed looks. *Well,* this *night is starting out really well!*

We followed Brooke into the house and stopped in the kitchen. Her mom was sitting at her computer and looked up. "Hi, girls," she said. "I'll be ordering pizza shortly. I'll let you know when it gets here."

I waited for Brooke to introduce me to her mom, but Brooke, Manda, and Lilly turned to go up the fancy staircase.

I walked over to Brooke's mom. "Hi, Mrs. Brennan," I said. "I am Livi. It's nice to meet you."

Mrs. Brennan turned her head in my direction but kept her eyes glued to her Candy Crush game on the screen. "Oh, uh… nice to meet you too. You girls have a nice time."

I caught up to the girls, who were already halfway up the stairs. Brooke and Manda were immersed in a conversation about pimply faced Ebony.

"Did you see the ugly jeans she was wearing today? Where did you get those? The bargain table at the flea market? And, *eww*…her hair looked like she hadn't washed it in a month!"

Lilly and I followed them and reached the top step together. Lilly glanced at me and gave me a half smile. She looked as though she felt as uncomfortable as I did. She kept her eyes focused on the carpet.

We reached Brooke's room. I was amazed at how big it was. A massive, white four-poster bed took up almost one whole wall. A tall matching dresser and a desk lined the opposite wall. A floor-to-ceiling mirror on one wall reflected the neon-pink room. The one large window by the bed was draped in zebra stripes as was the quilt at the foot of Brooke's bed. A zebra-striped sofa with a matching chair made a comfy sitting area in one corner. There were several pink and zebra-striped pillows strewn around the room. Over the head of the bed, large black wooden letters spelled "Brooke." A large-screen TV was mounted high on the wall opposite the bed. Several posters decorated the walls. One was a bold print of a pair of black and white polka-dotted high heeled shoes that were trimmed in neon-pink. Another had an abstract painting of a cool, brown-haired girl dressed in a trendy fashion; along the border was written "Diva."

I continued to scan Brooke's exquisite room, and my eyes were drawn to a poster of a rainstorm. It was simple and magnificent all at the same time. The rain was being whipped around the silver-gray, stormy sky. The message was written in white and almost disappeared into the picture:

> *Life isn't about waiting for the storm to pass.*
> *It is about learning to dance in the rain.*
>
> —Vivian Greene

I was mesmerized by the message; I couldn't pull my eyes away from it. Suddenly, I realized that the room had become silent. I forced my eyes to break away and turned to see Brooke, Manda, and Lilly staring at me.

"*Hel-looooo!* Earth to Livi. Where did you go?" Manda said, laughing.

I told them I was just amazed at how beautiful Brooke's bedroom was. And I told Brooke that I really, *really* loved the poster about the rain. I didn't tell her that it spoke to my heart.

"Thanks," Brooke said, and laughed. "Being an only child has its advantages."

I suddenly realized that I, too, was now an only child. And I couldn't think of a single advantage. With my next breath, I felt an overwhelming sadness fill me. I missed Mom, Dad, and Ivy. I fought to hold in the tears.

Brooke and Manda did not appear to notice my struggle, but Lilly seemed to recognize that something was wrong. I was grateful when she started to unroll her sleeping bag.

"When do we eat?" she asked. "I'm starved! Brooke, maybe you should check with your mom to see when the pizza is getting here."

Brooke headed for the door. "Good idea," she said. "I'm starved too." Manda followed Brooke, and they ran out of the room and clomped down the stairs.

I was still feeling pretty uneasy after Brooke's little prank—and pretty embarrassed.

After a moment of awkward silence, Lilly said, "That was pretty mean of Brooke to do that to you. I could tell you were embarrassed." I was not completely sure if she was talking about my jumping out at them on the porch.

Suddenly, Lilly jumped in front of me and yelled *"Boo!"*

"There," she said, laughing. "Now we're even." I didn't know how to take her gesture. Lilly plopped down on her sleeping bag and sat cross-legged. She looked up at me and whispered, "Brooke has a habit of doing stuff like that. I have learned to not let her see that it upsets me when she does it to me."

I plopped down on the floor, crossed my legs Indian-style, and whispered, "Why does she do stuff like that? It made me feel so awkward. She was the one who said we should scare you guys. But when she gave me the sign to do it, she backed out. I really felt like an idiot. I don't even really know you and Manda, and I felt like a fool."

Lilly and I locked eyes. "You'll learn how to handle it," she said. "I keep telling myself that Brooke doesn't mean anything bad when she does stuff like that to me—but it *does* hurt my feelings. Sometimes I wish that I could be like Brooke. It is just so easy for her to talk to people. I…well…I kind of have a hard time with that."

"Yeah," I said. "Brooke has been really nice to me. She kind of rescued me a few times since my first day of school here. And it was really nice of her to invite me to spend the night with you guys."

Lilly smiled with her lips tightly closed; I got a feeling that she wanted to tell me something—but I could have been wrong.

We heard Brooke and Manda clomping back up the stairs, and we smelled a wonderful aroma.

"Pizza!" Brooke announced. She was balancing two large pizza boxes on her head, and Manda was loaded down with paper plates, napkins, and bottles of water.

I jumped up to help them unload. "I'm starved!" I said, just before my stomach let out a large growl for all to hear.

"Oh my God, Livi! I guess you *are!*" laughed Manda. All at once, we burst out laughing—and couldn't stop. The harder we tried, the more we laughed. Brooke snorted. Manda burped. Lilly got the hiccups. And for the first time in a long time, I was laughing. I was suddenly having a great time—and I didn't feel guilty at all.

After our feast, we stuffed the dirty napkins, plates, and water bottles into the two empty pizza boxes and then collapsed onto our individual sleeping bags.

"Ugh," Brooke moaned. "I am so full!" We all moaned in agreement. Brooke reached over, picked up a remote, and pointed it at the light switch over by the door. The lights in the room slowly dimmed and then went out entirely. Brooke's electric alarm clock emitted the only light in the whole room. The display read 7:10 p.m. The numbers cast an eerie blue-haze reflection in the floor-to-ceiling mirror on the wall next to us.

Brooke sat up and pulled her sleeping bag over her head like a hoodie, leaving only her face exposed. She flipped on a tiny flashlight she had hidden under her sleeping bag and shone it up and onto her face. The small beam of light cast shadows onto her face and made her eyes look like two black and empty holes. She tossed a flashlight to each of us. We each sat up, and we pulled our sleeping bags over our heads. We shone our flashlights onto our own faces.

"It is time, my pretties," Brooke said, cackling like a witch, "for the truth-or-dare hour." Manda and Lilly groaned in unison. "You must tell the truth, the whole truth, and nothing but the truth." Brooke continued in a haunting whisper, "Failing to do so will result in your demise." Brooke shone her flashlight onto Manda's face, then moved it onto my face, and then onto

Lilly's face. *"Do I make myself clear?"* she shrieked, cackling once again. We all jumped and burst into nervous giggles.

Brooke then flashed the beam of light directly into Manda's eyes. "Man-daaaaaaa," she whispered, "tell us whooooo you would like to kiss on the lips. And remember, to lie will result in a painful *death*!"

Manda gasped, opened her eyes wide, and pretended to be frightened. "Well...I hate to say this, but...I think the answer to that question...is...I would most like to kiss...on the lips... Bobby Hendry!" Manda lay down and covered her face with her sleeping bag. "Oh my God! I can't believe I just said that!"

"Oooh, Man-daaaaaa!" Brooke said, and she and Lilly laughed. "Really? Bobby Hendry?"

Manda came up from under her cover and said, "I think he is adorable—and so smart. I'd kiss *him* on the lips any day of the week!"

"He *is* cute," I agreed.

Can't say that I'd want to kiss him on the lips, but he is cute. Can't say that I know any boy who I'd like to kiss on the lips.

Once we settled down, Brooke resumed. "Lil-leeeee," she said, "tell us the boy whooooo you would like to be stranded with on an island." Brooke shone the flashlight only inches from Lilly's face, cackling and snorting. "You must tell the truth and nothing but the truth. To lie will result in your untimely *death*!"

Lilly giggled and pulled her face back from Brooke's. "I must say, Brooke, you are really creeping me out."

Brooke leaned in even closer. "Just give us your answer, Lil-leeeee. Your life depends on it."

Lilly continued to giggle. "Okay. Here goes. If I were stranded on an island, I would like to be stranded with...Bobby Hendry!" We all burst out laughing.

"Well," Manda said, pretending to cry, "you can't have him! He is mine! All mine!"

"Wow!" I said. "What is so special about Bobby Hendry?"

I had to admit that I had noticed his dreamy blue eyes. And I had been a little embarrassed, but pleased, when he gave me his seat on the bus ride home a few days ago. "Here, Livi," he had said as I searched for an empty seat, "you can have mine." I noticed that he squeezed in next to pimply faced Ebony, who was sitting a few seats away.

Brooke became serious again, leaned into me, and shone the light straight into my face. "Liv-eeeee," she whispered. I could smell her pizza breath. "What is the scariest thing that has ever happened to you?" Manda and Lilly sat up straight.

"Oh, *this* ought to be good!" Manda said, laughing.

"You must tell the truth, the whole truth, and nothing but the truth," Brooke cackled, "or you will die! Did you hear me, Liv-eeeee? I said you will *die*! Hee, hee, hee!"

I knew this was just a game, but I didn't know what to do. I didn't know how to answer that question. I didn't know if I should tell the truth—or if I should lie.

I was never good at lying. Ivy used laugh at me. "Livi," she had said one day, "why in the world did you tell Mom that it was you who stained her sweater? She had no idea that you even borrowed it, and she already said that she must have spilled spaghetti sauce on it. Boy, Livi—you're too honest for your own good. A little white lie will never hurt anyone." Well, Ivy was probably right, but still—a lie was a lie was a lie.

Brooke was becoming a little impatient. "You must tell us *now*, Liv-eeeee. What is the scariest thing that has ever happened to yooooou?" Manda and Lilly were silent—waiting.

I took a deep breath and then exhaled—and I began my tragic story. I went back there—to Sutcliffe, Massachusetts, the Cape, on July tenth, the day my mother, father, and sister were killed in that car crash by a drunk driver. I relived every moment since then: The wake. The funeral. The burial. The move to Chelsea, Connecticut, to live with my grandmother and grandfather. The devastation I felt. The loneliness and hopelessness. The fear. The anger.

When I finished, I realized that my face was soaked with tears, and my nose was running. I really felt like I had been *away*. I heard the sobs of Brooke, Manda, and Lilly. The blue light from the clock across the room read 10:12 p.m.

"Oh my God, Livi. I had no idea you were dealing with all of that. Oh my God, I am so sorry. I don't know what to say. I am just so, so sorry," Lilly said, wiping her eyes. Her nose was running too.

Manda tried to speak, but she had lost her voice. She just leaned in and hugged me. And then Brooke did the same. And then Lilly. I don't even know how long we stayed in that group hug. I only know that it felt warm and comfortable. I never, never, *never* thought I would feel that close friendship—that bonding—again.

But as my dad used to say, "Never say never, Livi."

9

On the ride home, I told Grammie all about my sleepover: about Brooke's little prank; about how stupid it made me feel; about the brief talk Lilly and I had; about Brooke's gorgeous room; about the pizza; about the spooky truth-or-dare game; and about how I had spilled my guts and told them every detail surrounding the tragic deaths of Mom, Dad, and Ivy, including how I had to leave my home in Sutcliffe to make my home in Chelsea.

"Wow, Livi, an awful lot happened in one night!" Gram said. She looked concerned. "Are you okay, sweetie?"

I sighed. "I don't know how I feel, Grammie. I kind of feel that I shouldn't have shared everything. That maybe I should have waited awhile—like until I knew if I even trust these girls. I kind of feel disappointed in myself for letting my guard down too soon." I looked over at Grammie, who was driving with both hands clenched onto the steering wheel. "Why do I feel so uneasy about this, Gram?" I asked as I gulped back tears.

"Well, sweetie," Gram said, glancing over at me, "maybe you felt pressured to share more than you were ready to share. You shared some very personal stuff. But maybe talking about it—getting it out in the open—will help your heart heal a little quicker. And maybe, as you get to know these girls more, you will trust them and feel safe with them. It sounds like all three girls were genuinely moved by your story and were genuinely trying to comfort you. Sometimes, when we let our guard down and spill our guts to someone, a sacred bond forms. And that can be something that lasts forever." Grammie reached across and squeezed my hand, and then she pulled it up to her lips and kissed it. "I love you, my sweet Livi. I am very proud of you for fighting your way back from that awful place you were in."

"Thanks, Gram. Yeah, I guess you're right. The girls seemed as sad as I was. And they were crying as bad as I was. Our group hug seemed to last forever. It felt so good—for all of us, I think." I looked out the window, but I didn't see anything. In my mind, all I could see was Ruby; I really wanted to talk to her. I would have given anything if I could have used my thinking rock right about then.

We pulled into the driveway, and Grammie parked the car. As if she had read my mind, Grammie said, "Why don't you give Ruby a call? I bet she is missing you as much as you are missing her. You could run all this by her, and maybe she can help you sort through all of these feelings. You have always trusted Ruby with your heart."

I just smiled at Grammie, and the tears started to well up in my eyes. "I think I will do that." This time I reached over for Grammie's hand. I picked it up, brought it up to my mouth, and planted several kisses on it.

"Love you!" I said as I climbed out of the car. I grabbed my backpack and sleeping bag and headed for the back door. I looked back, and Grammie was still sitting behind the wheel. I started to head back to the car, but Grammie looked up and waved me off.

"I'm okay, Livi. I just need a few moments alone. You go ahead—and tell Ruby I said hello."

I saw that Grammie was crying. But I knew that sometimes it helped to cry—to get feelings out. So I gave her some space, some alone time. I had lost my mom, my dad, and Ivy—but so had Grammie.

I went into the house and headed straight for the phone. Papa was napping on the couch, "watching" a football game. I quietly picked up the phone from its charger and carried it up to my room. *Oh, Ruby, please be home. Please, please, please be home.*

No luck. But just as I was about to end the call, I heard Ruby's voice. "Hello?" she said.

I shrieked into the phone. *"Hiiiiiiii!* It's me!"

A split second later, I heard Ruby's squeal. *"Hiiiiiiiiii!* Oh my God! Livi! I was just thinking about you! Oh my God! Oh my God! *Oh my God!* Are you okay?"

I assured her that I was okay. "I just miss you sooooo much! And I miss home! And everyone from home! How are *you?*"

I plopped down on my bed. My cheeks hurt from smiling so much. We covered all the news there was to cover. Ruby caught me up on everything. I told her all that had happened to me since I had moved away from Sutcliffe. I told her about Brooke, Manda, and Lilly. Ruby asked a million questions, and I answered each one as best as I could before we wandered off into another topic. We were cramming over two months into one conversation. I felt so normal and so loved. *How I miss this. How I miss Ruby.*

"Oh, I miss you so much, Rubes," I told her.

"Oh, Livs," she said, "I miss you too. It is just not the same without you here. I'm so sorry that you are having a hard time. I know how much you miss your family. I miss them too. They were my second family. Every time I walk past your house, I say a prayer for you—and for me—that somehow things get better. I sometimes go to your thinking rock in the dunes, and that makes me feel closer to you. I hope that somehow we can have a sleepover weekend soon—either here or there—because I miss you so much."

We finally hung up after promising each other that we would work on making that sleepover happen soon. I set the phone down and sighed. Part of me felt wonderful. And part of me felt even sadder than before, because I was not sure that our weekend would ever really happen. Sutcliffe was not on the other side of the world, but it was a three- to four-hour drive— on a good day. If the traffic was bad, well, that was another story.

I felt I should take out my journal, but I was just too exhausted. We hadn't gotten much sleep last night. After I bared my soul to Brooke, Manda, and Lilly, I had lain awake, listening to their quiet breathing, envious that they could fall asleep so easily.

I knew I should go and take a shower, but I was just too tired. I thought that maybe I would just close my eyes for a minute.

I woke to Papa's deep voice: "Hey, Livi! Olivia! Come on down to dinner, sleepyhead." He laughed. "Boy, I take it you didn't get much sleep last night!"

I moaned, stretched, and smiled up at Papa. "Dinner?" I couldn't believe that I had been sleeping for five hours. "Okay," I said, yawning.

Papa kissed my cheek and tweaked my nose. "Grammie made her famous fried chicken," he said. "Come and get it." That was all the motivation I needed. I suddenly realized that I was starving. I popped up from my bed, raced past Papa, and practically flew down the stairs into the kitchen.

"I knew *that* would get you!" Papa said, and he laughed.

10

Mr. Griswold's gruff voice bellowed over the PA system in homeroom. It was 8:05 a.m.

"Just a few reminders, students," he said. "First of all, there will be an early dismissal Friday—tomorrow—at 1:10 p.m., so your teachers may begin parent-teacher conferences. Secondly, check the bulletin boards in your individual homerooms for information about cross-country sign-ups. That will be happening next week, so if you're interested, you'll need to get all the appropriate information. Okay, everyone—that's it for today. Have a great day!"

The bell rang, and we scrambled out of homeroom. I didn't know the two boys or the one other girl who stood with me in front of the bulletin board. We bobbed back and forth as we each tried to see the notice about cross-country sign-ups. I jotted a few notes down on the cover of my math workbook. Sign-ups were next Thursday at three o'clock in the gym.

I remembered that I hadn't gotten around to bringing up that subject at my sleepover with Brooke, Manda, and Lilly. Thinking of them, I wondered why I hadn't really heard much from them since that time. There had been a few hellos when we passed each other in between classes. But I had only managed to sit with them once on the bus all week, and the only reference to the sleepover was Lilly's comment when she said, "How are you doing, Livi? That sleepover was a real emotional night, huh? I keep thinking about you and your story."

Before she could say anymore, Brooke had interrupted. "Hey! Who has the homework assignment for Mrs. Manning's social studies class? I spilled my chocolate milk all over my notebook at lunch. What a mess!"

I was not sure, but I had sensed that Brooke purposely interrupted us—like she didn't want us talking about the sleepover or about my story. But that didn't make any sense. Brooke had seemed genuinely touched by my story, and it appeared that she had enjoyed my being there. I even felt that we four had formed a bond. I was confused by the turnaround. And Manda had been acting odd too—looking away whenever I made an attempt to start a conversation with her. *I just didn't get it.*

Later, as I walked to the cafeteria for lunch, I couldn't get my mind off of their strange behavior. I felt myself going into a funk. Had I done something wrong—something that upset the girls? I was oblivious to my classmates, who were rushing past me so they could get a good seat. It was fried chicken day. The cafeteria always filled up quickly on fried chicken day, unlike meatloaf day when the cafeteria was nearly empty and the ice cream line was long. I saw Lilly up ahead, and she was walking alone too. I took a chance and ran to catch up with her.

"Hi, Lilly," I said as I fell into step beside her.

Lilly jumped. "Oh, hi, Livi," she said. Too late, I realized she had been crying. Now I *really* felt awkward.

"Is something wrong, Lilly?" I asked cautiously.

Lilly waved off my concerns. "I just have a bad cold," she said, and sniffed. "I must look pretty bad."

"Well, you don't look *bad*, Lilly, but you do look *sad*," I said. "Are you sure you are okay?"

Lilly attempted to answer me, but the tears began, and she was swallowing hard trying to keep them in. She covered her eyes with her hand. I didn't know what to do. I scanned the area. The baseball field was just behind where we were standing.

"There's no one over on the bleachers, Lilly. Do you want to go sit over there for a little bit? I'm really not all that hungry anyway." She avoided eye contact and just nodded. I followed Lilly, and she settled on a bench halfway up. She sat with her back to me. I sat next to her.

I was trying to think of something appropriate to say when Lilly burst out crying.

"Oh my God, Lilly," I said as I put my arm around her back. "What *is* it?" After several attempts, Lilly, still sobbing, began.

"First of all, Livi, let me say how sorry I am that we have been ignoring you. I feel so bad about that! I know you noticed that we were, but I didn't know what to do. I am not a mean person, but I feel like what we've been doing is just so mean. Please forgive me, but I just don't know how to handle this!"

I was blown away. I had been hoping that it was just my imagination that they were ignoring me—but to hear that my gut feeling was right all along, well, I was seriously blown away. I didn't know what to say.

"Did I do something to make all of you mad?" I asked. "Is it because of what I said during the truth-or-dare game? It was the truth, Lilly. Do you, Brooke, and Manda think I made it up? Oh, Lilly, I thought we were all becoming friends, but I guess I was wrong. I'm so sorry if I upset all of you." Then I began to cry. I felt desperate and defeated. I felt worthless and alone.

"Oh, Livi," Lilly said, turning to face me. Now it was her turn to put her arm around *my* back, "*You* didn't do anything wrong! You were just being honest. I know Manda feels bad too, but—" Lilly looked away, wiping her eyes on her jacket sleeve. "But," she continued, "Brooke is just kind of weird sometimes. She *has* to be the boss. She does that to me and Manda sometimes; some days she likes me and talks bad about Manda or wants me to ignore Manda. And some days she likes Manda, and they both ignore me. It doesn't make any sense. But Manda is kind of a misfit, like me. We both started school here last year, shortly after Brooke did. Neither of us had any friends, and Brooke sort of adopted us. For a little while I was thankful, but then, after a while—once everyone knew that Manda and I were Brooke's friends—no one bothered with us. And now you are in the same club that we are."

I stared at Lilly in amazement. I had never experienced anything like this before. It never entered my mind that things like this happened. I just assumed that any friends I might make here at Chelsea Middle School would be like the friends I had at home—like Ruby.

The warning bell rang, alerting us that we had to be in our next class in five minutes. "I guess we better go" was all I could think of to say. I got up to leave.

"Can I walk with you?" Lilly asked. Her voice was hoarse. She was no longer crying, but her eyes were red, and she sounded all stuffy.

I just shrugged my shoulders. We walked together, side by side, but said nothing. I started up the steps of Shaddock House where my English class was held.

"I guess I'll see you," I said to Lilly. Lilly half waved to me and continued on. Her eyes were downcast. Just as I pulled open the heavy wooden door, Lilly called my name. I turned and looked at her.

"Can I phone you after school?" she called to me.

Again, I just shrugged my shoulders. "I guess," I said as I ran into the building. It felt good when I let the door slam behind me.

Mr. Ballou frowned at me, but said nothing as I slid behind my desk a moment after the final bell had sounded. No one seemed to notice that I had been crying. We had a vocabulary quiz in English, so my classmates were hunched over their papers.

Give the definitions of the following words and then use them in a sentence.

The first word was *attentive*.

I had studied the night before, and I knew I would breeze through this quiz.

Paying attention, I wrote. *John was attentive during the movie.*

I was feeling sad and confused after my talk with Lilly. I was aware that I really was not all that *attentive* right then, but I forced myself to *pay attention*. I finished the quiz, walked it up to Mr. Ballou's desk, returned to my seat, and then put my head down on my desk. I glanced up at the big clock above the door. Only fifteen more minutes, and then I could go to gym class. I wondered what we would be doing. Last week we had played volleyball, and our team had won. It was fun to play something as a team. Slowly, I had been meeting some new kids. Maybe it was time to try a little harder to make some new friends. I was not so sure I liked where this was going with Brooke, Manda, and Lilly. My heart felt so sad because, out of the three of them, I had been beginning to like Lilly the most. For some reason, I felt more at home with her. But now I didn't know what to feel.

Why does she want to call me tonight? I wondered. I was just so confused by all of it.

The bell rang loudly and jolted me out of my thoughts. I collected my things, stuffed them into my backpack, and headed for the door. I was so lost in my thoughts that I was heading down the stairs in the gym before I came back to reality. I took a deep breath and blew it out. I was looking forward to gym class.

I found out that we would be running. Miss Curtis said she wanted to encourage us to sign up for cross-country. She was telling us about the health benefits of good diets and exercise—especially running. I listened intently about the Chelsea Wildcats and how they had placed third last year. I was really excited to go outside and begin. Now, *this* was something I knew about. Last year had been my first year of cross-country running, and, from the beginning of the season to the end, my coaches were pleased with my progress.

"Keep it up, Livi," Coach Smith had said one day, after a good run near the end of the season. "You could become a star player on the team. It takes discipline and perseverance, and you *can* do it." He patted me on the back. "You just need to keep at it."

Miss Curtis and Miss Jaynes led us through the drills. They were watching us and timing us. When class was almost over, Miss Curtis asked, "Anyone want to do a few laps around the field?" I raised my hand immediately. "Okay, Livi!" she said. "Anyone else?" I felt embarrassed because I was the only one who wanted to do it. Then, someone raised a hand behind me. I turned to look, and I saw that it was Ebony—pimply faced Ebony—who really didn't have any pimples at all. She was not much taller than me, but she had legs that wouldn't quit. "Okay, Ebony!" Miss Curtis said. No one else raised their hand.

Miss Curtis had us stand side by side on the dirt track that circled the field. "Okay, girls. Let's see what you got." The rest of the girls sprawled out on the grass and got comfortable. Miss Curtis raised her arm up in the air. "On your mark…get set… *go!*"

Ebony and I started out. Soon I was lagging behind as Ebony zoomed ahead, but I was running steady, saving my energy. We completed one lap, and Ebony was still about ten strides ahead of me. The class cheered, giving us encouragement. I even heard a "Go, Livi!" When we were halfway into the second lap, I noticed that Ebony was starting to tire. I continued to run steady and soon passed Ebony. When I completed the second lap, Ebony was about ten strides behind me. I found my groove and continued to run. I felt good—elated—and I continued to run steady. I forgot about Ebony, about the rest of the class, and about Miss Curtis and Miss Jaynes; I forgot about Brooke, about Manda, and about Lilly. I was thinking only of Mom and Dad and of Ivy. I could hear them cheering me on—and I ran steady. I completed my third lap and then my fourth. Before I could continue, Miss Curtis waved me down.

"Okay, Livi! That was great!" she said. "You look like you've done this before!" I slowed down gradually and stopped, bent over with my hands on my knees, resting for a minute. I heard my classmates cheering, "Way to go, Livi!" I got some pats on the back.

Ebony came over to me. "Wow, Livi, you are really good. You left me in the dust!" She was smiling, and we high-fived. "I haven't run since last year, and I am obviously out of practice. I hope you plan to sign-up for cross-country. We sure could use you on the team!"

I told her that I did plan to sign-up, that I had run cross-country for the first time last year at my old school, and that I was really looking forward to running again.

"Well," Ebony said, "maybe we could start running together this weekend to get ready for next week's tryouts."

"That would be great!" I told her. We agreed that she would phone me the next night so that we could make some plans.

"Well, I sure am glad to hear that!" Miss Curtis chuckled. "See you both next Thursday for tryouts—three o'clock in the gym." As she walked away, she said, "Okay, ladies. Head for the showers."

Pimply face Ebony and I ran off the field together and headed for the gym.

11

Wednesday, September 24

Dear Ivy,

So much has happened in just one week. I can't stand the roller-coaster life I lead now! One minute I'm up, and then Boom! *I'm down. I don't know who to trust. I don't know who my friends are—or even if I have any friends. Of course, I still have Ruby—I'll always have Ruby—but it is just so awful not being able to have Rubes in my life here. I talked to her last Sunday after my sleepover, and it was like we had never been apart. I just miss her so much. I miss seeing her and talking with her every single day, like we used to in my old life. To be honest, I am so afraid that we'll never be able to see each other again.*

Anyway, Ivy, this whole thing with Brooke, Manda, and Lilly is so upsetting. I know that now that you are in heaven you can look into my heart and feel exactly how I feel, so I don't have to go into detail here. I just wish you were here to tell me what to do about it all. I know you are up there smiling down at me because I have made up my mind to try out for the cross-country team at school.

I love you, Ivy—and I will love you forever! Say hi to Mom and Dad, and give them a big hug and a kiss from me, okay? (And from Buffy too!) Tell them I am trying really hard to be good. I wish we could all be together again!

Love,
Livi

At dinner, I told Grammie and Papa all about my day. I could tell they were very happy that I had decided to try out for cross-country next week. I told them that Ebony had suggested we get together over the weekend so that we could go running. I hadn't heard from her yet, but I was pretty sure she would call. I hadn't heard from Brook, Manda, or Lilly either. I couldn't get Lilly's face out of my mind—or the conversation we had had—and I found myself feeling sorry for her, even though she hadn't yet called like she said she would.

After dinner, it was still pretty light out, so I told Grammie I was going up to the Hideaway. I hadn't spent much time up there over the past few weeks, and I felt like I needed to be alone; I needed to think about all that had happened.

I climbed the rickety stairs and pulled the light cord that only barely lit up my corner of the attic. The sun hadn't set yet, and it shone in through the window at the end of the room. It cast long shadows over my secret parlor and made it look somewhat eerie. I settled down into my red velvet chair, inhaled deeply, and then sighed. The past few weeks had been crazy, but all in all, I thought I had survived them pretty well. My mind wandered, and I found myself staring at the crack that zigzagged across the old mirror leaning against the eaves. I was mesmerized by the way the sunbeam struck the crack and then split into several little rainbows. I couldn't draw my eyes away. In my mind, I began to see visions of Mom, Dad, and Ivy. They appeared just the way I remembered seeing them just before I had left for that sleepover at Ruby's on the night before they died. I felt like I was right there with them.

I was smiling when I suddenly realized where I was. The warm feeling, the glow of being with them for those moments, lasted for a few more seconds. It felt so good. I looked up to heaven—where I was sure they were—and just sighed. I knew they knew what I was feeling right then, what was in my heart. I looked back down at the crack in the mirror, but the sun had already begun to set, and it no longer filled the space with light. The long shadows had begun to fade. Again, I sighed. I pushed myself up and out of the chair. As I walked past my table, I gently ran my hand over my paint brushes and made a mental note to begin a painting—maybe Sunday if nothing was going on. Grammie hadn't called up to me to tell me I had a phone call, so I guessed that Ebony had changed her mind about getting together over the weekend. I decided that I would go running by myself on Saturday. There were lots of woods and trails in the woods behind Grammie and Papa's house—my house—and that would be good training for cross-country. I headed toward the light at the top of the stairs, pulled the cord, and carefully felt my way down the attic stairs. Just as I was closing the door, I heard Papa calling me.

"Livi? *Livi!*" he shouted up from the kitchen. "Where *are* you?"

I yelled down from the hall, "I'm right here, Papa. What's up?"

Papa told me I had a phone call. I ran down the stairs to the kitchen and into the den. I picked up the phone—not sure whose voice I would hear, Lilly's or Ebony's.

"Wow! Where were you? Your dad was looking all over for you." I recognized Ebony's raspy laugh. I didn't bother explaining that that was my grandfather who was looking for me, and I didn't explain that I was up in the Hideaway.

We spoke for a short time, and I told her about my plan to run the trails behind my house on Saturday; I asked Ebony if she wanted to join me.

When I hung up, I was grinning from ear to ear. Ebony's mom would drop her off at my house Saturday morning around ten. I was overcome by relief. And joy. I told Grammie and Papa that I was going to my room so that I could get my outfit ready for school.

"I am going to go to bed early tonight," I told them, "so I'll say good-night now." When I got to the stairs, I turned back to them. "That was Ebony on the phone," I said. "She's going to come over Saturday morning, and we're going to go running in the back woods—we're starting to condition for cross-country. I hope that's okay."

I saw the quick smiles that Grammie and Papa exchanged.

"Good idea!" Grammie said. Papa was gazing into the opened refrigerator. He gave me a quick thumbs-up as he nibbled on a leftover chicken leg.

I ran up the stairs two by two and laughed as I heard Grammie say, "You keep eating like that, Joe, and you're going have to sign-up for the cross-country team too! I don't know where you put it!"

12

"Let's start down this trail," I suggested. "I have no idea where it leads to or how the terrain is."

I explained to Ebony that the land behind our house was part of an enormous land preserve, which meant that it had to be maintained by the state of Connecticut and that it would always remain as forest—open to anyone who might want to enjoy the beauty of it. It also meant that no one could ever buy it to build on it. Grammie said that meant it would forever be Mother Nature's sanctuary, and it could never be spoiled by humans.

The morning air was a little brisk—perfect for running. The sky was blue, and there were no clouds in sight. The trees along the trail had begun to change to red, orange, yellow, and gold, and we both welcomed autumn with a big sigh. We were silent for the first five minutes as we conditioned our breathing and strides. Ebony spoke first.

"This is absolutely beautiful, Livi! Boy, I wish I had this behind my house!"

I told Ebony how I remembered it—how, over the years, I had walked on these same trails with Mom, Dad, Ivy, Gram, and Papa. I told her how we would pack a lunch and hike for a while and then stop by a brook to eat. I told her it had been a while since I had done that.

"I have no idea which trail leads to that brook," I said. Our breathing had evened out, and it was easy to talk as we ran. We were again silent for a few minutes. The only sounds we heard were the birds chirping above us and the crunching of the leaves and acorns that blanketed the trail under our feet.

"I'm confused, Livi," Ebony said. "Don't you live here?"

"I do now," I explained. "It's a long story."

"Well," Ebony chuckled, "I *do* have all day."

Once again, I was hesitant to tell my story. It seemed that ever since I had told Brooke, Manda, and Lilly about the circumstances surrounding the death of my family, things had soured between us. But I didn't know how to keep it to myself, and I didn't know why I should. It was a part of me now, and it was nothing to be ashamed of. Everyone had tragedies of some sort in their lives, and this just happened to be mine.

I started from the beginning. Every now and then, one of us would point to a new trail, and we would change our course. Ebony listened intently, only interrupting occasionally with "Oh my God, Livi, I had no idea" or "Oh, Livi, I am so sorry" or "Oh, Livi, how terribly awful!" I heard Ebony sniffling. Out of the corner of my eye I saw her wipe her nose on her sweat-shirt sleeve. She continued to remain mostly silent, and I knew that she was listening to my every word. After I was done telling my story, we continued to run side by side in silence. I was lost in my own thoughts, and I guessed Ebony must have been too.

From a distance, a faint trickling sound broke the silence. We continued on the trail, and gradually we heard splattering and then loud babbling as the brook's waters rushed to cascade over and around the rocks and branches within its banks.

"This is it!" I exclaimed. "This is the brook I was telling you about!"

"Why don't we stop for a bit?" Ebony said, more a statement than a question.

"Really?" I asked, "You don't mind? We really have a good run going."

"Believe it or not," Ebony said, looking at her watch, "we've been running almost an hour already. We don't want to overdo it. It's our first time out this season. And, remember—we still have to run *back* to your house."

We trotted a short distance and then stopped and caught our breath.

"Oh my God, Ebony! This is the exact same spot where we used to picnic—the place I was telling you about!" I looked around and couldn't believe my eyes. It was as if time had stood still. The same fallen oak tree lay parallel to the brook, only now almost no bark remained. It had weathered and was now silvery white and silky smooth. The brook had widened some over the last few years and was barely a foot away from the tree. Tall spruce and oak trees cast a cool damp shade over the large clearing—and the ground was covered with the same velvety-moss carpeting that I remembered. A few of the sun's rays poked through the treetops and radiated down to the shady area where we were standing. Above the gurgling of the brook, we heard the sounds of a blue jay squawking and the rustling of leaves made by two squirrels that were foraging for their next meal.

"Wow!" Ebony whispered. "This really is sort of majestic! Mother Nature at her best. I can see why it is such a special memory to you."

I was overwhelmed for an instant as I thought of the last time I was there. I had a quick vision of Ivy and me sitting on the fallen tree. We were each eating a Granny Smith apple, and Ivy suddenly jumped up screaming. She had a trail of tiny red ants climbing up her bare leg. She was jumping up and down and hysterically trying to brush them off. She was shrieking at us, "Will somebody *please help me*?" We were all laughing, and that was only making Ivy furious at us. Finally, Mom, still laughing, was able to get to Ivy to help her brush off the last few ants.

"Great!" Ivy had whined as she tore off her sneakers and jumped into the brook. "Glad I wasn't dying or anything!" She was bending down and splashing water all over her legs. "I suppose you would have laughed at that too." A few moments later, Ivy was laughing right along with us. And that just made us laugh all the harder. What a wonderfully silly memory. I hadn't thought of that in some time—probably not since it had happened two years ago, I guessed.

"Are you okay, Livi?" Ebony asked. "Looks like you went somewhere else for a second."

I smiled and shared my memory. "Seems like just yesterday," I said. "I am so glad we found this spot today."

"Well, I am glad too, and I am honored that you are sharing it with me," Ebony smiled.

Ebony was lean and muscular and only a few inches taller than me. Her hair, which hung just to her shoulders, was black and looked a little wild; little wet ringlets currently framed her face. Even in the shade of the trees, her hair was so silky that when the sun's rays poked through and struck it, the black turned to blue. Little streams of perspiration trickled down her forehead, temples, and above her top lip. Her skin was smooth—like porcelain—and white, in sharp contrast to her black hair. Feathery jet-black lashes flattered her violet eyes, which were almost luminous. Ebony was a natural beauty, and I sure didn't see any evidence of the pimples or greasy hair that Brooke and Manda had spoken of.

"Let's sit and put our feet in the water," Ebony suggested, already bending to unlace her sneakers.

"Good idea!" I agreed.

"*Ahhhh*," we said in unison. We stood in the ice cold water and cautiously lowered ourselves onto the fallen tree. "Oh, that feels so good," Ebony sighed. I just moaned in agreement.

We sat in silence for a moment, side by side, and enjoyed the beauty that surrounded us and the cool relief felt by our feet.

"This is great, Ebony," I said, breaking the silence. This time it was Ebony who moaned in agreement. "I don't just mean how great this cold water feels," I began. "I mean this is great: you and me, running and talking."

"I'm really glad we got together, Livi," Ebony said as she leaned back on her elbows and turned her face up to the bit of sunlight that had begun to shine directly onto us. "Funny, but I feel like we have known each other forever."

"Me too!" I said. "You know, I've told you a lot about me, but you haven't told me anything about you. Have you always lived here in Chelsea?"

Ebony told me that she had only moved to Chelsea two years ago from California. "I was really upset when my dad—who is in the navy—told me that he was going to be stationed in New London, Connecticut. We bought a condo in Chelsea, on Bean Hill, only a half hour from the base. At first, I hated everything: the move, our condo, fifth grade at Chelsea Middle School—just *everything*. It was really hard trying to make new friends at a new school, especially starting fifth grade in the middle of the school year. There were a few kids who were really mean to me—you know, girls who called me *fat*, called me *ugly*, or just ignored me. But then, last year, I joined the Chelsea Wildcats and found out that I loved running cross-country. And I met a lot of new girls who are really nice. Moving around a lot like I have has made it hard to ever really find a 'best friend.' It seemed like everyone already had a best friend—do you know what I mean?" Ebony was still leaning back on her elbows, but she had turned to look at me.

"Yes! I *do* know what you mean. I know *exactly* what you mean," I said, and I found myself telling Ebony all about my recent experiences with Brooke, Manda, and Lilly. Told her how sad it had made me feel—how confusing and disheartening it was. "I think I am a nice person, so I don't understand why they've treated me like that."

We sat and talked and talked and talked. The whole while, we gently kicked our feet back and forth in the water and lapped up the warmth of the sun poking through the tall trees above us. We exchanged stories and were amazed at how similar they were. And how similar *we* were.

Clouds began to fill the sky, and the temperature dropped. Leaves of all colors began to fall like snow as the gentle breeze became a light wind. We decided to head back to my house.

About halfway home, we were pelted by a sudden, brief rainstorm. By the time we reached my house, we were both soaked to the skin. When we reached the back porch, we kicked off our sneakers and peeled off our socks. Grammie poked her head out.

"Oh, you girls are soaked! You must be freezing! Come on in, and get out of those wet clothes." She held the door opened for us as we shivered our way past her. "Let me go get a couple of robes for you two," she said. "You can both warm up while I put your clothes in the dryer."

Gram came back into the kitchen with two fluffy white robes. Both were delightfully warm.

"Here," she said. "Now, go into the laundry room, and get out of those wet things and into these nice warm robes that I just removed from the dryer. I knew you were going to come back soaked to the gills!"

"*Mmm*," we both said as we walked back into the kitchen.

"Oh, these feel so good! Thanks, Gram," I said as I kissed her on the cheek.

"Yeah, thanks, Gram," Ebony said, and laughed and kissed Grammie on the cheek too.

Grammie burst out into a hearty laugh—something I had not heard her do in a very long time.

"How about if I make you each a big bowl of chicken noodle soup?" she said. "That will warm you right up."

"*Mmm*," we said again.

"That sounds wonderful!" I said, and nodded to Ebony, and she followed me up the stairs that led to my room.

"I just love this old house, Livi. I feel like I have been here before. I know I haven't, but it just feels like I have. Like I told you, Livs, I feel like I have known you forever."

No one—except for Ruby and Ivy—had ever called me "Livs." Somehow, I felt like I had known Ebony forever too. I was smiling on the outside, but more importantly, I was smiling on the inside too.

13

Ebony and I had just plopped down across my bed when Papa knocked on my opened door and then poked his head in. He had the phone held tightly against his chest.

"I don't know who it is," Papa whispered, "but she sounds like she is crying. Do you want to take this?"

I shrugged my shoulders and looked questioningly at him. "I guess I better," I said.

Ebony whispered, "I'll go wait for you downstairs, Liv."

I put one finger up. "No, wait," I said.

"Hello?" I answered. I wondered whose voice I was going to hear. All I heard was someone sniffing, and a hoarse voice trying to speak. "Who *is* this?" I asked. I was starting to become worried that this was going to be very bad news.

Between sniffles, I finally heard her say, "It's me, Livi—it's Lilly. I'm sorry to call you like this, but I didn't know who else to call."

"Lilly?" I said, surprised. "What's wrong? What's the matter? Are you okay?"

"Oh, Livi," she said. She sobbed, sniffed, and then took a deep breath. "I really need a friend."

"Okay, now, Lilly," I said, trying to sound calm, "take a deep breath, and try to tell me what is wrong. Why are you so upset? I *am* your friend."

Lilly began, slowly and hesitantly at first. But the more she talked and confided in me, the more comfortable she seemed to feel. She spoke mostly of Brooke, and through her sobs I was able to piece her words together and figure out that Lilly was feeling left out and rejected by Brooke—and hurt that Manda seemed to go along with Brooke's hurtful words and behavior.

Ebony was sitting right next to me on my bed and could hear Lilly's every word. She looked at me, put her hand over her heart, and seemed genuinely sad for Lilly. "Why don't you tell her to come over?" Ebony mouthed to me. "Would that be all right? She sounds really upset."

I nodded in agreement. "Lilly," I said, interrupting her, "Ebony is here right now—we went for a run to get ready for cross-country tryouts. Is there any way you could come over here? Right now? We could talk all this over. Sometimes just talking to someone helps. Please, come over. We would really like to help. You sound so upset, and you don't have to be alone. Please, come."

"Really?" Lilly seemed surprised. "Really, Livi? You sure you don't mind? I'm sorry to bother you and Ebony. Do you think it would be all right? I mean…with Ebony there and all… I'm sorry to intrude…I—"

I stopped her. "Lilly, it is Ebony's idea for you to come over. You are *not* intruding. Let's just say we are friends helping a friend. That's what friends do, Lilly."

Ebony nodded to me. I held the phone out toward her. "Honestly, Lilly," Ebony said to Lilly from where she sat. "We want you to come over. Maybe we can help you sort this out. You know what they say: three heads are better than one."

While Lilly went to check with her dad, Ebony and I sat quietly.

"Poor Lilly," Ebony said, breaking the silence. "I know what she is going through—been there, done that. It hurts."

I was about to agree when Lilly came back on the phone. "Dad said he'd drive me over there right now. He knows where you live. I should be there in about twenty minutes."

"Great!" I said. "We'll be waiting outside on the front porch."

"Okay," Lilly said quietly. "And...Livi?"

"Yes?" I was just about to hang up.

"Thanks. And thank Ebony too."

We hung up.

I looked gratefully at Ebony. "Thanks," I said.

Ebony waved her hand at me. "Livi, you're welcome. But we both know—we are just doing what friends do."

14

The sun was setting outside my bedroom window. Long shadows crept across my room. Ebony and I lay across my bed and listened intently to Lilly, who sat cross-legged on the floor. She was leaning against my closet door with shoulders slumped, clutching a box of tissues. Crumpled-up tissues were strewn on the carpet around her. Buffy lay curled up next to Lilly, resting her head on Lilly's leg. As Lilly told her story, she seemed unaware that she was gently stroking Buffy's neck. Every now and then, Buffy lifted her head, looked up at Lilly, sighed, stretched, and then snuggled a little closer to her.

"I moved here last year, only a few weeks after Manda did," Lilly began, and then stopped to blow her nose. "I have always been really shy, and it has always been hard for me to make new friends. My father's job as a sales manager means he has to move around a lot—and that means that I do too. I've moved four times since first grade, and that means that I have had to start at a new school and try to make new friends four times. Each time, it just got harder. Some kids were just mean to me and called me awful names.

"At my last school—in Ohio—when I was in fifth grade, a bunch of girls started calling me 'skinny ginger kid.' 'Hey, skinny ginger kid, cat got your tongue?' 'Hey, ginger kid—if you stand sideways and stick out your tongue, you'll look like a zipper.' I don't know why they hated me so much. I never did anything to them. I was too embarrassed to tell them to stop.

"They started following me home from school every day. Over time, the teasing got worse. I was too afraid to tell them to stop—so I said nothing at all. One day, I thought that if I got a head start on them as soon as we got out of school, I could run all the way home and avoid them all together. Well, that didn't work; they chased me all the way home. This happened every day after school, but what they didn't plan on was me outrunning them. Every day I got faster and faster, and finally I could leave them in the dust. They'd still yell out mean things to me as they passed by my house, and I'd peek out at them through my bedroom window, praying that they would keep going.

"Just when I thought I couldn't stand it anymore, my father told me that we were moving." The longer she talked, the faster she spoke. "For the first time, I was glad to hear those words. I was happy, because I thought that starting a new school would be my chance to finally make some friends. When I first started at Chelsea Middle School last year, I met Manda—who was kind of shy like me but so nice—and I thought things would be better."

"Whoa, Lilly," I said. "You need to breathe. Take a deep breath; you're going to make yourself sick." I got off the bed and lowered myself down onto the floor next to Lilly. Ebony did the same. We both hugged her. Lilly then rested her head on my shoulder.

"Well, what happened with Manda?" I asked.

"Well," Lilly said, and then hesitated, "it's almost like Brooke snatched up Manda—then me—and then kind of took us under her wing. Like she knew we both were shy; we were the new shy girls in the class, and she sort of adopted us. We both thought Brooke was really well liked—popular—and so we both were grateful that Brooke was helping us to get accepted by the kids.

But then I realized that Brooke was bossing us around and playing us against each other. One day she'd be nice to me and mean to Manda, and then the next day she'd be nice to Manda and mean to me. And I have to admit, because I didn't want to be the one left out or the one she was mean to, I kind of found myself being mean to Manda too. Some days, Manda was mean to me, but I understood why she was. She was just trying to stay on Brooke's good side. I know this makes me sound crazy—like a bad person—but I'm really not like that. I hate that I was being mean to Manda. And I hate that I let Brooke treat me and Manda like that."

Lilly blew her nose again and sat quietly for a few seconds before she continued. "And now I feel like no one in the whole class likes me. And I don't know what to do." With her head slumped on her chest, Lilly said softly, "Livi, I called you because—for some reason—I feel that you are the only one who can help me. I feel like I can trust you." Lilly looked up at the ceiling, took a deep breath in, and then blew it out. "I just feel so alone. I can't talk to my dad about this. He's Mister Big Shot in his company, and he's always too busy with his meetings and dinners. He's barely home. I get so lonely; I have no one to talk to—ever."

"What about your mom?" Ebony asked. "Can you talk to her?"

"Oh, I thought you knew: my mom died two years ago—she had cancer." Lilly closed her eyes, and I saw a tear trickle down her cheek. "My dad hasn't been the same since."

I looked at Lilly. Her eyes were swollen, and her nose was red. Her cinnamon-red hair—usually meticulously styled—was tousled, bedraggled, and pulled back into a lopsided ponytail. Today's rain had caused tiny ringlets to form around her face.

"Oh, Lilly," I said, "I am so sorry about your mom. Why didn't you tell me? You listened to my sad story at the sleepover, and you never said a word about your own sad story."

"Crap," Ebony said. "You are breaking my heart, Lilly. I just want to hug you!"

"Me, too," I said. And, again, we shared a group hug. "Feel the love, Lilly! Feel the love!"

Lilly began to cry. "I *do* feel the love! You and Ebony are so nice! It means so much to me that you asked me to come over, that you listened to me...that...even after all I've told you, you both are still so nice to me!"

Ebony and I both began to cry along with Lilly. "Boy," I said, "we must be quite a sight. We're all teary and snotty nosed."

With that said, we all began to giggle, and then, before we knew what had happened, we were rolling on the floor laughing uncontrollably. We shared a sweet release. Mountains of crumpled-up tissues were piled around us in the dark. By now, my Big Ben clock across the room read 8:35 p.m. "I think I should ask Grammie if you two can sleep over," I said. "What do you think?"

An hour later, we had joined Grammie and Papa in the kitchen. Sitting around the big oak table, we laughed and told stories as we gobbled up ice cream sundaes. I could tell that Grammie and Papa were enjoying themselves just as much as we were. And I knew that somewhere up above us, Mom, Dad, and Ivy were smiling too. They had to be happy that there was so much love in that kitchen: Grammie, Papa, Ebony, Lilly, and me—and ice cream sundaes—at 9:35 p.m. on a Saturday night.

15

By the time I got to the gym, I was out of breath. The huge clock said it was 3:10 p.m., and I was ten minutes late. Miss Curtis and Miss Jaynes had already begun to give instructions to the girls who, like me, wanted to try out for the cross-country team. I immediately felt nervous and looked around the room for Ebony. She saw me first. I calmed down as soon as I saw her frantically waving at me from across the gym, and I trotted over.

"Hey!" I said, still out of breath. I explained that I was late because Mr. Tauro had wanted to talk to me after class.

"Is everything okay?" Ebony whispered. She bent to tie her sneaker laces. "I just got here too."

"Yeah," I whispered back. "He actually told me he was pleased with my work. And he asked me how things were going—if I was adjusting okay to Chelsea Middle School."

Ebony was about to respond, but Miss Curtis approached the area where we stood.

"Okay! Ebony and Livi! Glad you could make it!" she said. "You both had me worried; I thought you had changed your mind about running this year." She shot a big smile at us and told us to go over to where Miss Jaynes was working with a group of girls.

The first person I saw when we joined the group was Brooke. She was staring at me.

"Well, look who's here," she said. "I didn't know you were interested in running, Livi. You never said anything about it." Then she turned and realized that I was with Ebony. "Hey, Ebony," she said as she brushed a strand of her long brown hair out of her eyes. With that, she turned, and her ponytail swished against my cheek. "Oh, sorry," she said, without looking at me.

I leaned away from the swinging ponytail.

Brooke now looked me straight in the eye. "I didn't know that you and Ebony knew each other," she said.

Before I could answer, Miss Jaynes's whistle commanded our attention. Our entire group of ten girls hushed and listened intently to what was expected of us at the day's tryouts. It was then that I realized that the girls who I was standing with had all been on the Wildcats cross-country team last year. Miss Jaynes introduced me to them.

"Okay, girls. Even though you were on the team last year, you will still have to run to see if you qualify. Livi here," she said as she put her hand on my shoulder, "was on her cross-country team in Massachusetts last year. I have seen her run, and if she does as well today as she did last week, I think she'll be a great addition to our team." Miss Jaynes motioned for us to form a circle around her. "Now, head outside. You know the route through Spaulding Park. My staff will be timing you on the course. Good luck—and I'll talk to you when you return."

Our voices echoed in the gym as we left. Ebony and I walked together, and Ebony explained that the park, which was back-to-back with the school, was owned by the town. "There are lots of great trails and paths that run through it—but no brooks, like in your little piece of heaven," she said, laughing.

Brooke caught up to us and fell into step beside us. "Gee, Livi," she said, "you are just full of surprises. Hope you can keep up."

"Oh, I don't think Livi will have any trouble keeping up with any of us," Ebony answered. "She is awesome."

"Humph," Brooke said, without looking at either of us. "We'll see. I hope you're right." Brooke trotted off to the starting line. Ebony and I were right behind her.

As we were stretching, several of the girls high-fived me and wished me luck.

"Hope you make the team, Livi."

"Sounds like you are just what we need, Livi."

"Hey, Livi! Nice to meet you!"

I watched as all the girls, one at a time, also acknowledged Ebony with either a smile or a high five.

"You are standing with one of our star runners, Livi. Ebony is awesome!" one of the girls said.

Ebony's smile was broad and natural. She beamed but remained quiet and humble. "We're a team, guys," she said, blushing as she resumed her stretching.

Brooke joined us. Ebony turned to her and high-fived her. "And Brooke here had the best all-around times last year. She is hard to beat."

Miss Jaynes raised her hand in the air. "Get ready, girls. See you at the finish. Good luck!" The whistle signaled for us to begin.

The trail twisted and turned and led us into the heart of the park. Ebony and Brooke took the lead early. My breathing was off, and I got a slow start. I was at the back of the pack with only one girl behind me, and I could hear her gaining on me. I began to worry; at this rate, I would not qualify.

Suddenly, I heard Ivy's voice in my head: *Control, Livs! Slow down your breathing. You got this! You don't have to prove yourself to anyone.*

I tripped on a tree root and fell to my knees. That slowed me down even more, and now I was the last runner in the pack.

So you tripped. Pay attention. I am telling you—you got this. Just do this for yourself, for Mom and Dad, and for me. Forget everything else, Livi. We know you can do it. And once you believe you can do it, you will. Now get the lead out and run!

Later I would debate with myself whether I had really heard Ivy's voice or whether I had imagined it. But, right then, I knew that what I heard—or what I thought I had heard—was accurate. I knew that Ivy was right. I could do it.

I focused on my breathing and slowed it down. Then I looked up ahead and visualized myself passing all the girls ahead of me. I focused all my energy on my stride and started to gain on the girl in front of me—and then the next girl, and the next, and the next, and the next, until there were only four girls ahead of me. Two were Brooke and Ebony, and they were running neck and neck, approaching the finish. I heard Ivy again: *Give it all you got, Livi! Kick it into high gear!*

Out loud, I heard myself saying, "I got it, Ivy!" I got a burst of energy and passed one more girl before I hit the finish line. I had placed fourth out of our pack of ten.

"Yeah, Livi!" I heard Ebony yell. She was bent over with her hands on her knees but ran over and hugged me. We jumped up and down. "You were great!" Ebony said, still jumping up and down. "That's what I'm *talkin'* about!" By then, our entire group had finished, and there were high fives and backslaps going around.

The other girls who were trying out were now starting to cross the finish. Off to the side, I noticed Lilly standing alone. When she saw me, she started to jump up and down.

"Woo-hoo, Livi!" Lilly shouted. "Woo-hoo, Ebony!" When she realized that Brooke had turned to look at her, she shouted, "Woo-hoo, Brooke!"

I wondered where Manda was. I scanned the crowd, but I didn't see her. I shot a thumbs-up to Lilly. The shriek of Miss Curtis's whistle silenced our celebration.

"Great job, everyone! I want to commend all of you for coming out today. Tryouts will continue tomorrow for those who couldn't make it today, so if you know anyone who might be interested, tell them to get here tomorrow after school. On Monday, I will be posting the list of those who made the team. It will be hanging on the bulletin board in the gym lobby. Good luck, everyone!"

As Miss Curtis and Miss Jaynes walked by me, each gave me a thumbs-up. "Good job, Livi," they said in unison.

I felt good—satisfied. I had managed to overcome my fear, and I was pretty sure that I would make the team. I had done it for me, and I had done it all by myself—for me, myself, and I—with a little help from Ivy.

I looked up toward the sky and smiled. *Thanks, Ivy.*

16

By the time we got back to school, there were only a few strag-glers on campus. I gathered my books and stuffed them into my backpack. My legs were covered with the dust and dirt that I had kicked up during my run. My blond hair, still pulled back into a long ponytail, was sweaty, dirty, and two shades darker than usual. I was dying of thirst and suddenly felt very hungry. My knee had a small abrasion where it had grazed the ground after I tripped on the tree root. I glimpsed at myself in the full-length mirror as I left the girls' bathroom in the gym. I was a mess, but I felt wonderful!

I made my way to the area where Grammie had said she would pick me up. I sat on the green wooden bench, which was somewhat sheltered by a massive oak tree. Most of its leaves had fallen, and they formed a golden-brown carpet under my feet. The autumn air had a chill in it, and I began to shiver. *I should have listened to Papa this morning. He said I should bring a coat because the weatherman said the temperature was going to drop this evening.* I pulled my sweatshirt sleeves down over my hands. There was a silence in the air that felt delicious. I inhaled deep-ly and enjoyed the scent of nuts and autumn leaves. I began to think of Lilly. And Ebony. And Brooke. And Manda.

I had noticed earlier in the day that Manda and Brooke were walking to lunch together—and that Lilly was walking alone just ten feet behind them. I saw Manda turn and glance at Lilly and then put her nose up in the air and turn back to her conversation with Brooke. I saw Brooke and Manda laughing. Then they both looked back at Lilly, put their noses in the air, and, arm-in-arm, disappeared down the stairs into the cafeteria.

I saw Lilly put her head down, turn, and head toward the bleachers.

I wanted to go and hug Lilly. I wanted to tell Lilly, "You're not alone—they did the same thing to me this morning."

I had been in the school bathroom when I had overheard Brooke talking about me to Manda and a few other girls. "Livi thinks she's going to make the cross-country team," Brooke had said. "But I've got news for her. One good run doesn't mean she is assured of a spot on the team. Livi is such a snot. She thinks she is so much better than everyone just because she went to a hoity-toity school in Massachusetts at the Cape. Big deal!"

I had wanted to storm out of my bathroom stall and scream at Brooke and Manda: "*Hey! You can't do that!* You can't be mean to people—to Lilly or to me." But I stayed in the stall until they all left. I did nothing at all. When I saw Lilly heading toward the bleachers, I wanted to run after her. To let her know I cared. To let her know that we were better than that. To let her know that she had friends—two, for sure. To let her know that the bond that we had formed over the weekend—Lilly, Ebony, and me—was still in place. We were friends, and friends stick together. And we would work this out—together.

I had wanted to do and say all that, to comfort her, but it wasn't possible. I was already late for English, and I couldn't chance an unexcused lateness—with detention after school—with cross-country tryouts scheduled.

Lost in thought, I didn't even hear Gram's car pull up.

"Livi!" she called from her opened window. "You ready?" I flung my backpack over one shoulder and headed toward the car. I tossed it in the back and plopped down onto the front seat.

"Oh, what a day, Gram!" I moaned. "Wait till I tell you about it! What's for dinner? I am starving! Can you please turn up the heat? I'm freezing!" As I fastened my seat belt and got comfortable, I began telling Gram every detail of my day's events. I was only halfway through my story when we drove into the driveway. It continued through dinner. I finally finished by dessert.

Papa took a deep breath and blew it out. "Well, it sounds like you had quite a day!"

"Livi," Grammie said, "all you need to do is to continue to be true to yourself. To treat people the way *you* want to be treated. People will find that they love to be in your sunshine. You will see who your real friends are. Friends love and support each other—they don't hurt and try to undermine each other. But some people are so unhappy with themselves that they only feel better when they hurt someone else—when they try to bring someone down. They are blinded by their jealousy and inadequacies. Sometimes, they *can* be won over by love and kindness—and sometimes they can't. Sometimes, you just have to let them go."

We sat in silence for a minute. Papa said, "Here, here! And on that note, I am going to watch *Jeopardy!*"

I just looked at Grammie from across the table. Somehow, she always knew just what to say to help me sort out my feelings. "You make it sound so simple," I said, sighing.

"Oh, it's not simple, Livi," Grammie said as she got up and began clearing the table. "I know it's not simple, but you just have to trust yourself—trust *in* yourself."

I rose from the table and carted the dirty dishes to the sink.

"I just felt so bad for poor Lilly today," I said as I rinsed the dishes and loaded them into the dishwasher. "She always seems so sad, and I don't know how to help her—other than to keep making sure she knows that I am her friend." I closed the door and hit the start button, and the dishwasher came to life. "I wish I knew why Brooke has been so mean to Lilly and me—and why Manda just goes along with her."

"Well, I think you and Ebony make a good team," Grammie said. "And I think if you and she stick together, this all might just work out."

Gram gave me a hug and tweaked my nose. "I'll finish up here, sweetie. You go and finish up your homework."

Once in my room, I fell onto my bed. I suddenly felt exhausted—partly from running in the tryouts and partly from the emotional roller coaster I had been on over the past few months. Talking to Grammie had helped some, but I couldn't get rid of the overwhelming need to talk to Mom—and Ivy. Dad had never been much of a talker, but I missed his hugs and corny jokes. I missed everything about my old life.

I opened my social studies workbook and turned to page 28. Mrs. Manning had talked in class today about our upcoming assignment that was due by October tenth:

Pretend you are a travel writer. You are traveling to another country, and it is your responsibility to report important information on how to survive living in that country. Aspects to include are climate, social conduct, cultural traditions, and important laws.

Report your results as a magazine article instead of using a typical report format.

My eyelids felt heavy. I lay my head down on my book. Just for a minute, just for a second...

I was running in the park with Ruby. The sun was warm on our shoulders. We ran in silence except for the sounds of our labored breaths. We were side by side, running at exactly the same pace. We were smiling and content, not a care in the world.

Suddenly, rain began to fall. It was cold, and it hit our faces hard. I turned my face away from the rain, and when I turned back, Ruby was gone. Instead, Brooke was there, sneering at me as she passed by me, running like the wind. There was a flash of lightening, and, in that moment, I could see that Brooke had reached a point far ahead of me. The trail had become wet with mud, and my feet began sliding. I feared that I would fall. And yet, with the next flash of lightening, I could see that Brooke was running with no problem at all; she was nearly out of sight. I passed Manda, who was sitting in a mud puddle alongside of the trail. She was looking up at me. I couldn't tell if those were tears running down her cheeks or if they were raindrops. I knew if I slowed down, I would lose—but lose what? I didn't feel like I was in a race—I felt like I was running. But where? I just knew that I had to keep going forward. I knew that if I stopped, I would lose my chance to…to what? To win? I felt confused. I only knew that I had to keep going forward.

Then I saw Ebony standing behind a clump of trees. It was raining all around her but not on her. She stood in a bright sunbeam and smiled at me as I flew by. I couldn't stop. I had to watch my footing. I had to win. But win what? What was I afraid to lose? I tried to turn my head to see if Ruby was somewhere behind me, but I had to watch my footing. I couldn't lose my footing. I felt sure she was back there somewhere. I knew she was back there.

All of a sudden, I felt a warm breeze on my back. I sensed that the sun was breaking through the clouds. I was running on dry ground with no mud or puddles in sight. All I could see was Brooke running way up ahead of me. Every now and then, she would turn, look at me, sneer, and then turn back. She was winning. But winning what? Maybe this was a race. She turned again to look at me, but this time she caught sight of something behind me, and she had a look of horror on her face. Before I could turn to see what she had seen, there was a deafening clap of thunder, and a strong gust of wind whizzed by me. Lilly was running at full speed, and she had a look of panic on her face. Tears ran down her cheeks, and her cinnamon-red hair whipped behind her. Within seconds, she was far ahead of me. And then there was a roar—like that of a passing locomotive—that made my ears hurt. Three girls with ghostly white faces and black hoodies sped by me. We were in a wind tunnel. The air was heavy, and I could hardly breathe. I was certain they were chasing Lilly. I tried to scream Lilly's name—to warn her they were coming—but nothing came out. I could see that Lilly was running far up ahead of me. I saw that she was about to overtake Brooke. I watched as Brooke veered off the trail to make room for Lilly. Brooke slowed and eventually stopped. When I passed her, she was kneeling on the side of the path. She had her eyes shut tight, and she held her hands over her ears and shrieked as though she were in severe pain.

I was coming to the end of the trail. I passed Ruby, who just smiled at me and gave me a thumbs-up. I passed the three girls who had been in pursuit of Lilly. They had given up their chase and were walking off into the darkness of the deep woods. I passed Ivy, who was sitting on a branch in a beautiful pink dogwood tree—just like the one in our yard in Sutcliffe. She was dressed all in white and bathed in a golden mist. "I knew you could do it, Livs," she said, without moving her lips. I smiled up at her and felt warm in her glow—in her sunshine. I wondered what I had done. There was no finish line, and I thought that made sense because there had been no start line.

Up ahead I saw that the sun was shining brightly through the deep woods. For a moment it blinded me, and I put my hands over my eyes. When I felt the warmth of the sun on my shoulders and back, I took my hands down. There sat Lilly, on the bank of a raging brook. Beside her sat Ebony. They both had their faces upturned to the sun and their feet in the rushing waters. They seemed content and waved me over. I sat next to them and put my feet into the cold water. I, too, felt content. Across from us, on the opposite bank of the brook, sat Brooke and Manda. The sun streaked down on them, and they seemed content too.

I smiled as I watched Ivy disappear into the deep woods. The golden mist followed her and then dissipated into the darkness.

I awoke and found that I had drooled all over my workbook. My room was dark, except for the bit of October moonlight that streamed across my bed. I tossed my book onto the floor and slid under my quilt. I knew I hadn't even showered. I knew I was still dirty and sweaty from tryouts. I knew I hadn't finished my homework—I hadn't even decided what country I would write about.

But I knew what I had to do—I knew what Ivy was telling me to do—and I felt content.

Good-night, Ivy.

17

"Oh, I couldn't *do* that, Livi!" said Lilly. "There's just no way I could do that!" Lilly stomped away.

I ran and caught up to her. "Lilly, please!" I pulled on her arm. "I had a dream last night, and it all made perfect sense. Please, Lilly—please listen to what I have to say!"

We stood in the midst of kids, who skirted around us as they headed to the first class of the day. Lilly stared at me. She pressed her lips tightly together, jutted out her chin, and refused to budge.

"Lilly," I pleaded, "I really think you could make the team; my dream last night showed me that you're a natural. You said you had to outrun those girls every day after school. You said you got faster and faster each time they chased you home from school. It just makes sense that you use that talent and speed on the cross-country team. Don't you get it? Those girls did you a favor by forcing you to run so fast. And being on the team might be a wonderful way for you to get over your fears—of being alone, of being bullied, and of being sad all the time."

Lilly continued to stare at me. "Livi, please," she said, "I know you mean well, but I just *cannot* do that." Tears welled up in her eyes.

"Lilly," I said as I looked around us. There were now only a few kids running to their classes. "Please, think about it. Tryouts are today at three o'clock; they are meeting in the gym. Let me know if you decide to go. I'll go with you—for moral support." I hugged Lilly. "We both better get going, or we'll be late for class."

We turned to go in opposite directions. I turned back and watched Lilly run toward the Slater Building.

"Lilly!" I shouted. When she turned, I shouted even louder: "What have you got to lose?" I turned and ran at top speed to my social studies class in the Buckley Building. The bell rang just as I reached my desk and fell into my seat.

I didn't see Lilly for the rest of the day—not even at lunch time. I figured she was avoiding me or had decided to go home "sick" so that she wouldn't have to deal with me. I started to feel guilty for pressuring her to do something that she obviously was afraid to do. What right did I have to try to get her to do something she didn't want to do? On the other hand, as her friend, didn't I have the right to encourage her to do something that just might make her life a little better? I said I would be there to offer her moral support. It's not like I was throwing her to the wolves—or *was* I? Oh well, it was too late now. I had already forced my own opinions onto her. Poor Lilly.

The more I thought about it, the more I realized that maybe I was doing it for poor me—*poor Livi*. Maybe it was my way to get back at Brooke. If, somehow, Lilly could become the star of the cross-country team, maybe Brooke would back off and leave Lilly and me alone. Maybe Brooke would stop bad-mouthing me to some of the girls in our class. Maybe Brooke would stop trying to turn Manda against us. Maybe Manda would see that Lilly and I were really nice people who didn't deserve to be treated so meanly and so unfairly.

There was no practice after school, because the final tryouts were going on, so I took the bus home. Lilly was not on the bus, so I assumed I was right—she had gone to the nurse and had gone home sick. Brooke and Manda sat together at the back of the bus. I slid into the seat with Ebony and filled her in on my dream and on the talk I had with Lilly earlier in the morning.

"Geez, Livi," Ebony looked serious. "That was an amazing dream. It almost seems like it was a message from Ivy." Ebony's eyes were opened wide. "Livi, you're kind of creeping me out. Look. I've got goose bumps."

"Yeah, well," I said as I looked out of the window, "I guess Lilly didn't feel the same." I squirmed in my seat. "I'm afraid she will never talk to me again. I think I went too far. I was just trying to help." I jerked Ebony's arm. "*Did* I, Ebony? Did I go too far?"

Ebony hugged me. "Liv, you were just being a good friend. Sometimes friends have to take a chance and tell friends things that they might not want to hear."

I found myself staring out the window again. "Then, why do I feel so awful, Eb?"

"Listen, Livs. You said what you felt. You offered Lilly a possible solution to maybe make her life a little better. You really meant well. Lilly told you that she knows you mean well. So, I guess you just have to respect whatever it is that Lilly does or doesn't do. *We* will just have to respect what Lilly does or doesn't do. We are her friends—no matter what. So I guess *we* should let her know that we are there for her—no matter what. Poor Lilly probably doesn't have any idea that that is what friends do."

"Yeah, I guess you are right. She probably thinks that we don't like her anymore because she didn't have the courage to try out today." The bus jolted us as it stopped at the corner of Hickory and Elm Streets.

Ebony and I pretended not to notice Brooke and Manda as they squeezed down the aisle toward the front of the bus. They hopped off and turned to wave to a few girls up front.

"Humph," Ebony said, rolling her eyes.

"Humph," I said back.

Moments later, the bus jolted to a stop again. The doors hissed opened. "This is me," Ebony said as she hoisted her backpack onto her back. "I'll try to call you later so we can decide what to do about Lilly."

I watched out the window as Ebony turned to wave to me. I waved back and watched her begin her trek up the long sidewalk that led to her front door. The doors hissed closed, and as the bus started to move, it rumbled and jerked. I bounced in my seat as I reached for my backpack. My stop was coming up in a few minutes. There were only a few kids left on the bus.

"Hey, Livi," Bobby Hendry said from across the aisle. "I heard you did really great at cross-country tryouts yesterday."

I jumped when I heard my name. When I realized who it was, I felt my face flushing. "Oh, th-th-thanks," I stammered. My voice had suddenly gone hoarse.

"Well, good luck!" he said. He smiled, and his blue eyes sparkled like diamonds. He lifted his backpack over his head as he maneuvered himself down the aisle and down the steps. I watched him through the window and was shocked and embarrassed when I realized that he saw that I was watching him. He smiled and waved at me. I waved back.

"Well, *that* was awkward," I said, under my breath. And I felt my face flush again.

I raised my backpack to my chest and lowered my face so I could smile undetected behind it. All I could think about was what Manda had said at the sleepover in response to Brooke's truth-or-dare question: "I hate to say it, but...the person I would most like to kiss—on the lips—is Bobby Hendry."

18

I couldn't get Lilly out of my mind. I was worried about her. I really didn't know why I hadn't seen her at school all day. Had she been sick? Had she gone home, and that was why I hadn't seen her on the bus after school? Had I made her mad because I was so persistent—so pushy—about her going to tryouts today after school? Had I crossed the line? I really wanted to call her after dinner, but I was afraid I might find out that she never wanted to speak to me again. So, I decided to give her some space. But I really was hoping that she would call me and let me know that everything was okay between us.

Out of desperation, I decided to go up to the Hideaway. I had been so busy with school and running and tryouts that I hadn't visited the attic in two weeks. A quick look around convinced me that the only thing that had changed was the thin layer of dust that had accumulated on my art table. With my finger, I wrote my name in the dust and drew a smiley face. I made a mental note to bring up a can of Pledge and a dust rag the next day. I also made a decision to begin a painting in the morning. I wasn't sure what I would paint, but I hadn't painted anything in far too long—since a few months before the tragedy happened. Had almost three months gone by since that tragic day? It seemed like a lifetime had passed—and basically, it had. My old life seemed deep in my past—and my future seemed impossible to see.

I sighed and realized that I really didn't feel like staying up in the attic anymore that night. The daylight was shrinking fast, and I really didn't enjoy the Hideaway after dark. I made a pact with myself that in the morning I would hold to my decision to start a painting.

Once back down in my bedroom, I curled up in my rocking chair by the window. I wrapped myself in Mom's Snuggie and Dad's flannel shirt. And I lay my head on Ivy's purple, heart-shaped pillow. I realized that I was spiraling down into a funk. I couldn't explain it or put a real label on my feelings. I just knew that I had a huge empty place in my heart, a really bad feeling of homesickness—like the first time I had slept over at Ruby's house. That feeling had been irrational because I knew Mom and Dad and Ivy were only five houses down the street, and I knew I would see them in the morning, but nevertheless, I couldn't shake that sad feeling.

I felt the same way now, only I knew I would never—*never*—see them again. *Sorry, Dad, your "never say never" bit of wisdom doesn't apply here.* And with that thought, I began to sob—so hard that I thought I would vomit. Oh, how I missed them!

I missed Mom's sweet hugs and kisses, the constancy of her in my life, and her devotion to me and Ivy and Dad. I missed the way she always knew what to say and what to do to make us feel loved and wanted. I missed her unspoken promise that she would always be there for us. Even though she had been taken from me, I still felt her presence around me.

And Dad, oh how I missed my daddy! His smiles, his quirky sense of humor, and his corny jokes:

"Where'd you get your hair cut, Livi?"

"At Deb's Salon, Dad."

"Oh, yeah? I thought maybe you got it on your head."

Eyes would roll, and there would be lots of groans. But, that was my dad—always trying to cheer people up. He was always there if anyone needed help too. And he always kept his promises—he was a real promise keeper. If he said he would be there, he'd somehow get out of work in time for our events, games, concerts, and art shows. Even when his boss said he needed everyone to work overtime to finish a big project, Dad would make it on time. He never broke a promise to us. I missed smelling his cologne—Nautica—and I missed his laughing eyes and his teddy-bear hugs.

I missed Ivy. Beautiful, sweet, sassy Ivy. Although she was two years younger than I was—only days away from turning ten when she died—she was so very wise. She always seemed to understand…well, everything.

Mom used to say Ivy was an old soul, that she must have lived a former life. A few years ago, Mom and Dad had to deny Ivy's request for a horse: "Ivy, we only have one acre of land here; that is hardly enough for a horse to roam. And do you know how much money it would cost to feed a horse? And who do you think would take care of a horse while you're at school or away at camp?"

Ivy's answer was, "But, like you said, Mom—I'm an old soul. I think I lived a former life as a cowgirl, so I think it is only fair that you get me a horse—and a saddle, boots, and a cowgirl outfit." We all had a good laugh over that at the dinner table one Saturday night.

I missed so many things: the room that Ivy and I had shared, our talks that sometimes went well into the night, our walks on the beach, and the hours we spent riding the waves in the ocean. I missed everything about Ivy. I regretted all the times I had told her I wanted to be alone: "Ivy, please! I need some time to myself! Just me, myself, and I. Now, scram!" If only I could take those times back. If only I could have the chance to be with Ivy again—even just one more time. I would tell her how much I loved her and treasured her. I knew that she was in heaven now and that she knew exactly how I felt, but still, I would just like the chance to tell her that in person.

Slowly, I untangled myself from Mom's Snuggie and Dad's shirt. I got up from the rocker, tossed Ivy's pillow back onto my bed, and went to my dresser. I pulled open the drawer and fished out my diary from its hiding place. Despite the fading light, I opened it and began to write.

Friday, October 3

Dear Ivy,

There are no words to tell you how I feel—how bad I miss you and Mom and Dad. I don't know why it just seems to hurt so much more today than usual. I mean, it always hurts... bad...but today—tonight—I feel like I just can't bear it any-more. I want you to know that I love you, that I have always loved you so very much, and that I am afraid that you never knew just how much I loved my beautiful little sister. So right now, if you can hear me and feel what I feel, please know how very much you were—and are—loved. I wish there were a way for you to let me know somehow that you can hear me when I talk to you and feel my heart when it is missing you so bad.

Good-bye, for now.
Livi

19

I woke up Saturday morning with the sun streaming in on me. I stretched and rolled over onto Buffy. As I rolled off of her, I glanced at the clock on my nightstand and saw that it was 10:10 a.m. So much for getting an early start up in the Hideaway.

"Morning, Buffy-girl," I said as I scratched her belly. "Boy, I guess we both were tired, huh?"

"Okay! Time to get up!" I said, and rolled out of bed. Buffy rolled over onto her belly, put her rear end up in the air, and stretched from head to tail. She jumped off the bed and followed me down the stairs into the kitchen. "Where is everyone?" I asked Buffy. The house was silent, except for the loud ticking of the old clock that hung on the wall beside Grammie's antique faded-blue hutch. I spotted a note on the butcher block that told me that Grammie and Papa had gone grocery shopping and that I would find my pancakes on the plate by the microwave. I removed the foil covering, popped the plate into the microwave, and set the timer. Buffy waddled over to her doggie bowl and started to crunch on her own breakfast.

When the beep signaled that my pancakes were ready, I took them out of the microwave, poured a little maple syrup over them, and sat myself on the high stool at the end of the butcher block. I was facing the window that looked out to the front yard and the enormous copper beech tree. Its leaves were coppery-gold and shone brilliantly in the October morning sunshine.

The broad branches had only just begun to shed their copper foliage and spiny beechnuts onto the ground below. I sighed. I loved living in the country almost as much as I had loved living near the ocean. I felt peaceful this morning—contented. As I licked the syrup off of my fingers, I formulated my plan for the day.

I finished up my breakfast, grabbed a can of Pledge and a roll of paper towels, and headed back up the stairs to my room. I quickly straightened out my comforter, fluffed my pillows, and threw on my old sweats. Laden with the can of Pledge, paper towels, a set of new watercolor brushes, tubes of paint, and an old Cool Whip container of water, I carefully made my way up the attic stairs and over to the Hideaway. It was only eleven o'clock, and the morning sun was sending shafts of light from one end of the attic to the other. Under the eaves, the Hideaway was bursting with sunbeams.

"This light is perfect for painting!" I said to no one. I sprayed Pledge onto the table and, with a paper towel, wiped off the layer of dust. I was surprised how the beat-up old table gleamed in the sunlight. I arranged my big tote board onto the ledge of my wooden easel. With masking tape, I secured the edges of a large piece of Arches natural white, cold-press watercolor paper. I arranged my new paintbrushes in the recycled pickle jar and squeezed dollops of various colors of paint onto my palette. I was ready to begin.

I stood and stared at my blank paper. What to paint? My mind was as blank as the paper. I looked around the attic for some inspiration but found none. Every idea that came into my head didn't feel right. My head was suddenly filled with thoughts of Mom, Dad and Ivy, and there seemed to be no room for anything else. The excitement I had felt earlier was suddenly gone. I felt drained.

"Oh, this is just great," I sighed. I looked down at my palette full of paints: burnt sienna, cadmium yellow, cerulean blue, cadmium red, and viridian hue. "This is just wonderful," I said, shaking my head.

I let go of my paintbrush, and it plunked down into the glass pickle jar. I walked slowly over to the fancy wooden chair. Feeling defeated, I plopped myself down heavily onto the red velvet cushion, sending up a small puff of dust. I stared at my reflection in the full-length mirror across from me. The streams of sunlight bounced off of the glass and hit me square in the eyes; I had to look away for a second. But my eyes were drawn back to the mirror—and to the zigzag crack near the bottom. I was mesmerized by the hundreds of tiny diamonds that sparkled and radiated from the crack—beautiful shades of blue, violet, and red. I was spellbound by the magical display of lights.

I tried to ignore a sudden ringing in my ears and tingling in my entire body. But the ringing became so loud that I had to put my hands over my ears, and the tingling became so strong that I felt like my whole body was on fire. Everything was spinning around me, and I was becoming nauseous. The ringing in my ears got louder and louder, until I felt like my head was going to explode from the pressure. I tried to look away—away from the sparkling blues, violets, and reds—but I couldn't.

I heard a roar, then a thunderous rumble that sounded like a train was circling me. I felt like I was caught up in a tornado—spinning and spinning—while still trying to avoid looking at the sparkling diamonds of blue, violet, and red. I was helpless as the tornado spun me closer and closer to the brilliant lights. With a deafening slurping sound, and a *whoosh*, I was—in a flash—sucked into the depths of the mirror through the zigzag crack to a place I had never been before.

It took a minute for my head to clear, for my ears to stop ringing, and for my nausea to go away. My eyes were still closed, but suddenly I was aware of a radiant warmth that passed through my entire body. My senses were overwhelmed with earthy fragrances of honeysuckle, jasmine, chamomile, and alyssum. From what seemed like far away, I could hear a beautiful musical melody—a symphony of heavenly tones and chimes that seemed to be floating on the haze of pale-blue clouds that now encircled me. I was sitting alongside a shimmering stream that sparkled in the most splendid sunlight I had ever seen. As it trickled by, tiny ripples formed and made rings of dazzling aquas, yellows, and pinks in the foamy dark-blue water. I was stunned by the pure silence that blended with the enchanting music, and I was comforted by the overwhelming sense of peace that I felt in my heart and in my soul.

It didn't matter to me that I had no idea where I was. All that mattered at that moment in time was the sense of relief I felt. All that mattered was that I felt—for the first time in months—whole and completely content.

As the pale-blue haze started to lift, I began to see shapes and forms all about me. Green and gold trees swayed back and forth in time with the soothing musical chimes. Luminous hills rolled into the distance. There seemed to be no beginning and no end to any of this. But I didn't question it. I just knew—and enjoyed—that this was where I was meant to be.

I squinted my eyes to block the sunlight that was preventing me from clearly seeing a distant figure that was approaching me. It gradually took shape as it got closer. The shape seemed familiar to me, which made me feel comfortable and relaxed as it broke through the haze. It was a young girl who was bathed in brilliant sunlight. I recognized her walk, the way she swung her arms, and the way she turned her face up to the sun. She was only one hundred feet or so away from me, and I watched as she casually brought her hand up to her face and tucked a strand of golden-blond hair behind her ear.

"Ivy?" I said out loud. The sound of my own voice startled me for an instant. "Ivy?" I said again, a little bit louder. "*Ivy!*" I called as I stood and ran toward the girl. "*Ivy! Ivy! Ivy!*" I shrieked. My feet stumbled over each other as I raced to reach her. Ivy stopped for a second, and when she realized that it was me, she began to race toward me too. The gap between us became smaller and smaller until we crashed into each other, entwined our arms, and stumbled and fell onto the soft ground. We rolled around, still hugging each other, for what seemed like an eternity.

"Can this be happening?" I asked. "Is this possible?" Still lying on the ground, I took Ivy's face into my hands and studied it. "Is this really you, Ivy?" I couldn't look away. The sun caught the blue of her eyes and made her fair hair shine. "Oh my God, Ivy! How is this happening?" I began to sob. But I continued to look deeply into her eyes. It was as if our eyes were locked together.

Ivy sat next to me and cradled me in her arms.

"Yes, Livi, this is happening. This is real," she said softly. When I looked up at her, she gently wiped away my tears with her fingertips. When she smiled, the blue haze around us totally lifted. For as far as I could see, the sunlight washed over the rolling hills and seemed to wrap the trees in blankets of gold velvet. The stream's tiny ripples evolved into waves that crashed against the banks on either side. Ever so gradually, I began to hear a beautiful symphony of chimes that seemed to ride on the golden beams of sunlight.

I felt only joy—pure and simple joy. Still holding hands, Ivy and I helped each other up and stood facing each other. "I can stay here forever with you, right?" I said, more a statement than a question.

"Oh, Livs, no. This will be brief. Somehow, we are being allowed to spend this time together so that you may be reassured that who you are, what you are, and what you do is perfect. I know life for you now is filled with sadness, with confusion, and with hopelessness and fears. You are here now so that I can tell you that you need to keep on the path you are traveling. You are the kindest and most loving being I know, and you *will* figure out what to do—how to live your life so that you can find your destiny with joy. Just follow your heart, Livi—always follow your heart. You will see that everyone loves to be in your sunshine. I know you don't know that yet, but you will learn that eventually. Surround yourself with promise keepers—only promise keepers. You have so much love and truth to share with the world, Livi. That is why you were spared. That is why you were not in the car with Mom, Dad, and me on July tenth. You have much to do yet in your world. Your work is not done—it has only begun. Believe me, my dear, precious Olivia, the world—*your world*—needs you. Follow your heart. Share your truths. Dance in the rain."

"Where are Mom and Dad, Ivy? Can I see them too?" I scanned the golden hills and trees and the shimmering stream. "Please, can I see *them* too?" I begged.

"They are here with us, Livs. They have their arms wrapped around you. They want you to know that they are always with you, just like I am. It is like there is a lace curtain between our world and your world. When you need us, speak to us. We will hear you. When you want to touch us, reach through the curtain. We will touch you. You are never alone, Livi."

I began sobbing again. I felt my tears wash my face and spill onto my chest. I knew my visit in this place was almost over. The blue haze was moving in, surrounding Ivy and me. I held onto Ivy's hand tightly. I could no longer see her sweet face. The symphony of chimes was moving far back into the rolling hills, and I could barely hear any music at all. The trees were once again shrouded in the blue haze and clouds. The brilliant sunlight was fading, and dusk was approaching. The stream beside me was silent. The waves had dissolved into colorless ripples that had already begun to disappear into nothingness. The air that had once been warmed by the sun's radiance was now uncomfortably chilly. I no longer held Ivy's hand in mine, and I knew that she had gone. I wrapped my arms around me and eased myself onto the ground.

In my head, I could hear Ivy's sweet voice: "Follow your heart. Share your truths. Dance in the rain."

20

The attic was cold. I heard raindrops hitting the roof. I was curled up in the wooden chair, and the muscles of my back and legs were cramping. I moaned as I tried to untangle myself. My reflection in the mirror looked back at me.

Suddenly I remembered...remembered...what? Was it a dream? It couldn't have been a dream. It felt too real to be a dream. I closed my eyes and tried to picture everything I had just seen. I felt overwhelmed and stunned by my recollections: the magnificent sunlight, its remarkable warmth, the blue haze, the shimmering stream, and the golden hills and trees that swayed back and forth in perfect time with the celestial melody of chimes. And I remembered Ivy: being with Ivy, holding Ivy, Ivy wiping away my tears. Beautiful, radiant Ivy. Her hair had never seemed so golden, and her eyes had never been so pearly blue. There was an aura of brilliancy around her. I remembered the peace I felt. The comfort. The sheer joy and happiness. And then I remembered her words: "Follow your heart. Share your truths. Dance in the rain."

I stared at myself in the mirror for a long time. I kept going over all that I had seen and heard and felt—over and over and over again. I didn't want to ever let the memory fade. I kept trying to make sense of what I remembered. I kept trying to convince myself that it *had* to be a dream, that there was no way that what I remembered could have really happened. But it seemed too real to have been a dream. I studied my reflection in the mirror. I looked for any signs, any clues that might convince me—one way or the other. But I looked just the same as always. And the mirror looked just like it always had—zigzag crack and all.

Suddenly I began to shiver. I wasn't sure if it was because I was cold or because I was spooked. Maybe *spooked* wasn't the word I was looking for. I wasn't frightened. I didn't mind that I was alone in the darkened attic. I just felt confused and unsure—and yet hopeful that what I remembered was a real memory of a real happening. The only fear I felt was that maybe—most likely—it had been just a dream.

I had no idea what time it was. I thought I better go downstairs and check. I wondered if Grammie and Papa had returned home yet from the grocery store. My legs and feet had gone numb, and, as I rose from the chair, I felt pins and needles as my blood circulated back into my lower parts. I limped over to the stairs, but just as I was about to start down, the sun suddenly burst out, once again sending shafts of light throughout the attic.

The Hideaway was suddenly aglow with sunlight. A brilliant sunbeam pointed at my easel like an arrow. I was suddenly filled with an overwhelming urge to paint—but to paint what? To paint what I had seen in my dream? In my *happening*? It became astoundingly urgent for me to capture in my watercolors all that I had seen.

Without hesitation, I began. I worked feverishly as I mixed my colors to achieve the perfect blends of blue haze, gold mists, and sparkling blue water. As I moved my brush across my canvas, I could feel the energy and vibration of each stroke and, without even a conscious thought, I captured the exquisite beauty of Ivy and me as we looked into each other's face, as we clung to each other, afraid that if we let go we would lose each other forever. I used one paintbrush after another, dipping, dabbing, smearing, and washing. I watched as tiny droplets of paint ran down the paper—clotting and blotching—resulting in a softness of shadows and mystical illusions. Our golden hair faded into transparency, and our dresses of pearly white flowed daintily on purple breezes. It was as though I had stumbled onto a secret form of communication that let my soul speak to Ivy's soul. It was mysterious, and yet, I had never before felt so sure of anything in my life.

I signed my *Livi Breton* in the lower right hand corner of the painting. I stepped back to view my creation and gasped. What I saw was a miraculous image of celestial beauty. Somehow I had captured the magical scene that had been etched into my memory. I stood there in awe of my masterpiece—of my tribute to Ivy—and I began to sob. I felt such sweet release, such complete peace and accomplishment. I felt I had somehow reached a destination in my life. I felt I was experiencing a homecoming. I felt I didn't want to be anywhere else. Where I was in my life was exactly where I needed to be.

21

The rest of the weekend flew by. On Sunday, Grammie and I went to Morrison's Art Supplies and bought a beautiful gold frame. Papa matted and framed my creation, and we hung it in my bedroom on the wall between the two big windows that looked out onto the massive maple tree whose branches—now decorated with autumn leaves—twisted and turned upon themselves.

I titled my painting *The Visit*. Plain and simple. Grammie and Papa begged me to hang it down in the living room where it would be visible to everyone. They were in awe of the magical and mystical essence of my creation. I, cautiously at first, shared with them the recollection of my dream. Once I realized that they didn't think I was insane, I gave them all the details I could remember. They both agreed that something mystical had happened—whether it was a dream or a real happening. And they reluctantly agreed that the painting should hang in my bedroom.

I purposely didn't phone Ebony or Lilly over the weekend. I needed some private quiet time to sort out all the chaos that had been going on in my life over the past few months since I had started school at Chelsea Middle. I realized that I had begun to feel used and manipulated by Brooke. I came to the conclusion that she had attempted to "adopt" me—just like she had adopted both Manda and Lilly the year before—for the purpose—I believed—of making herself out to be the savior. She had "rescued" Manda first. She had seen that Manda was new to the school and somewhat shy. She had sensed that Manda was attempting to make friends with her new classmates, so, under the guise of being nice and being helpful, she befriended her. Soon after that, Lilly was new to the school, and Brooke saw that Lilly was very shy and somewhat intimidated and overwhelmed by the large number of kids in the sixth grade class. So Brooke befriended Lilly too. And then she was able to control both girls and limit their contact with the rest of the class.

Brooke manipulated the friendships she had with Manda and Lilly by playing one against the other—by one day being nice to one and ganging up on the other and then, on another day, turning it around and doing exactly the same to the other one. By that time, it was clear to the rest of the class that Manda and Lilly were "Brooke's girls." It slowly became clear to me that Brooke was not really well liked by the other kids in the class, and this was Brooke's way of developing a circle of "friends" around her. I think that both Manda and Lilly played right into Brooke's awful game because they were afraid that if they didn't, they would be left out of the circle. When Brooke decided it was a day to say mean things to Lilly, to snub her, Manda went along with it. And Lilly, when ordered by Brooke, would be mean to Manda and snub her. But Brooke didn't count on Lilly having a conscience and a loving heart. And Brooke didn't count on Lilly finding the strength to try to climb out from the abuse. Poor Lilly had spent months running away from the bullies at her other school. She had been tormented and shamed. And all she ever wanted was to live peacefully, be kind to others, and be a friend.

Brooke could be very nice at times. I had seen that for myself that first day on the bus when she "rescued" me. I was so grateful that someone had made an effort to become friends with me. I was feeling very lonely and pretty desperate on that first bus ride. And when Brooke offered to show me around campus and show me to my homeroom, I felt so relieved and hopeful that this might be the beginning of a nice friendship.

That sleepover at Brooke's house had been an eye opener for me. Looking back, I saw that there were several times during that evening that Brooke said or did little things that left me feeling uncomfortable and uneasy. I talked my way around those things, but deep down, I guess my gut was telling me to pay attention—to be careful. But it wasn't until that next week that I realized that I was being snubbed by Brooke, Manda, and Lilly. And I had no idea why—until Lilly poured her heart out to me on the bleachers that day. It was then that I realized the hard truth: Brooke liked to control our friendships so that we would do as she wished. She knew that we knew that if we didn't, we would be the one snubbed, the one on the outside looking in. I had listened to Lilly tell me about how Brooke manipulated their friendships, how Brooke knew that both Manda and Lilly had no other friends and had no one else to turn to; how Brooke knew that Manda and Lilly would turn back to Brooke for rescuing.

It had seemed so unbelievable and wicked when I first heard it from Lilly, but I was moved by Lilly's strong desire to share her feelings with me—to explain what she and Manda were going through, to trust me enough to pour her heart out to me that day on the bleachers, and to open up to both Ebony and me in the darkness of my bedroom. It was then—when I heard my own voice telling Lilly what true friends were, telling her that true friends didn't treat friends the way Brooke did—that I began to realize and determine that Brooke's "friendship" was not something I wanted in my life. It was then that I made a pact with myself that I was going to pursue new friendships and new activities that led me to those friendships. It was then that

I realized that it was up to me to take charge of me. It was time to start being nice to myself.

I had never had to work at making friends before. Ruby and I had met in first grade at Sutcliffe Elementary School and had become best friends immediately. And we thought we were the luckiest people on earth when we realized that we only lived a few houses away from each other. Our friendship was never tested. And even though we were best friends, we always invited others into our alliance. We both enjoyed the comradery of our entire group of friends.

I realized early on that Brooke wanted only a small group of friends, and she did not want us to invite anyone else into our little circle. That was when I began to feel inside of me that something was not right. I am not sure what gave me the strength to begin to pull out of Brooke's clutches. Maybe it was just talking to Ruby that helped me remember what friendship was all about. Maybe it was having Ebony enter my life at just the right time—and Lilly too. Maybe I was just beginning to learn to follow my own heart, my own truth. Maybe I was growing up.

My brain was on overload. But I felt better since I had gone through everything in my head. Things were starting to make sense to me. I knew the path I had to follow. I knew I had to help Lilly and Manda climb up out of the hole they were in. I knew I had to try to help Brooke too—if she would let me. My visit with Ivy had made so many things clear to me. I knew I was exactly where I was supposed to be, and I knew exactly what I was supposed to be doing.

Ivy said it best: *Follow your heart. Share your truths. Dance in the rain.*

22

On Monday morning, my heart was thumping out of my chest as Ebony and I approached the gym. The door to the gym lobby was propped open, and we could see the chaos inside. A herd of boys were jockeying for position as each tried to see the list that told which of them had made the boys' cross-country team. And the bulletin board directly across the small lobby was hemmed in by a throng of girls. Each girl was jumping up and down, trying to catch a glimpse of the list that would be cause for either her jubilation or discouragement. Several girls were standing on the fringe of the mob—some biting their nails and some just watching the lucky ones who were screeching and hugging other lucky ones. Every now and then, one of them would take a deep breath, quietly squeeze her way into the crowd, and get lost in the madness.

Ebony and I stood on the outskirts for a few minutes and held hands.

"Well, Livi," said Ebony, "it's now or never. You ready?"

"Yup," I said. I took a deep breath, blew it out, and yanked on Ebony's hand. "Let's get this over with!"

We waded in at first and then dove into the front line. We were silent as we started at the top of the list and read each name one by one. We both found our own name at the same moment.

"I made it!" Ebony screeched.

"Me, too!" I turned to hug Ebony. "Oh, Ebony! I did it! *We* did it! Oh my God! I can't believe I made the team! Oh my God! Oh my God! Oh my God!"

We wrapped our arms around each other and danced wildly around the lobby. Several of the other girls who had made the team joined in, and, before long, some of the boys, who were cheering for their own victories, started chanting in deep voices.

"Wildcats! Wildcats! Wildcats!"

Brooke had drifted near us, and when I went to high-five her, she glared at me and looked the other way. I looked wide-eyed at Ebony. "Did you see that?"

Ebony just waved it off. "I don't think Brooke is too happy about you making the team, Livi. I think she is worried that you'll give her a run for her money—no pun intended!"

I burst out laughing. "Well, I'm not going to let that spoil my mood," I said. "I am so happy! I still can't believe I made the team! I made the team, Ebony!" Ebony hugged me, and we danced around the lobby, joining the chanters.

"Wildcats! Wildcats!"

That's when I noticed Lilly standing alone in the dark corner. She had her hands in her pockets and a look of panic on her face. I pointed her out to Ebony.

"Lilly is here, and she looks like she is going to be sick."

We discreetly approached Lilly. She looked so pale and frightened.

"Lilly, what's wrong?" I asked delicately. "Oh, Lilly, are you okay?" I felt really worried that something awful had happened.

The crowd had begun to disperse, and the lobby was emptying quickly. The cheering and chanting soon faded away as the last few girls left. The heavy wooden door slammed shut, and suddenly the silence in the small room echoed in our ears.

"Lilly! Speak to us! What is wrong?" Ebony demanded.

We stood in silence. Lilly's breathing was rapid and loud. She inhaled deeply, puffed up her cheeks, and then exhaled slowly. She looked directly into my eyes and then turned and looked directly into Ebony's eyes. Very quietly, in almost a whisper, she said, "I made the team."

Ebony and I looked at Lilly in disbelief.

"What do you mean?" we both said at the same time.

"How could you make the team if you didn't try out?" I asked, confused.

"But, I did, Livi. I *did* try out. I listened to you, and I decided that you made a lot of sense. I decided that it was time I did something to change my life. I *did* try out after school that day—just like you asked me to. I went, and I was the only one there. Miss Curtis ran with me the whole way and cheered me on. I did really well, and I came in here early today before anyone else got here. I checked the list...and...and I made the team." Lilly looked from me to Ebony. She was no longer pale. She had a pink glow about her, and her blues eyes sparkled. She smiled a sheepish smile. "I made the team! *I made the freakin' team!*"

"Lilly!" I shrieked. "That is *awesome!* I am *so* proud of you!"

"Well, aren't you just full of freakin' surprises!" Ebony laughed. "Holy cow! This is just so awesome, Lilly! I am *so* proud of you too!"

We three wrapped our arms around one another and danced in a circle, chanting, "Wildcats! Wildcats! Wildcats!" Arm in arm in arm, we danced out of the gym, down the three steps, and onto the sidewalk. We strutted right in the middle of the walkway, causing everyone else to walk around us.

"What's the excitement all about?" several students asked as they passed by.

"We all made the cross-country team!" Ebony exclaimed. "It's a wonderful day!"

"Awesome!" they yelled.

And, indeed, it was a wonderful day. Ebony was just as ecstatic as I was, and we were both so happy and proud that Lilly had found the courage to try out—and that she, too, had made the team.

I floated through the rest of the day. I was still floating high when I got on the school bus at the end of the day. I couldn't wait to see Ebony and Lilly. They were sitting together near the back of the bus, and I hurried toward them. As I made my way up the aisle, several girls and a few boys—and Bobby Hendry—congratulated me.

"Thanks," I said, trying to be humble. When Bobby high-fived me, I blushed.

"Th-th-thanks!" I stammered. I wondered why I blushed each and every time he spoke to me. *Sheesh*, I thought, *if I were stranded on an island, I'd like to be stranded with Bobby Hendry.* "Congrats to you, too," I said, smiling a smile that was probably way too big. "I heard that you made the team too—again."

I plopped down in the empty seat in front of Ebony and Lilly. "What a day, huh?"

For at least the tenth time that day, we high-fived each other. We were basking in the glow of our achievements when I noticed Brooke and Manda staring at us.

I shouted up the aisle to Brooke, "Congrats! It's a great day, huh?" I didn't know what to say to Manda. She hadn't tried out for the team, and she had been avoiding me for several days. So I just smiled at her.

Brooke frowned. "Yeah, it's a great day for some of us. It's a real lucky day for the ones who didn't even try out and somehow made the team anyway." Her eyes drifted toward Lilly.

Poor Lilly was squirming in her seat and looking down at the floor. Once again, her face had gone pale. Brooke continued, "I don't think that is right. The rest of us had to try out and get a place on the team, fair and square. Do you think that is fair, Manda?" Brooke surveyed the kids sitting around her. "Do you all think it's fair that someone should make the team if they didn't even have the decency to try out? I personally think that stinks. How about you, Lilly? Don't you think that stinks?"

Brooke turned toward Manda. "You agree, Manda? Don't you think that stinks that Lilly made the team without even trying out like the rest of us?"

Manda looked taken aback and mortified. Those around her had gone silent. Their eyes had moved from Lilly to Manda.

"Uhhh…" Manda tried to speak. Her face was flushed. She looked over at Lilly. "Uhhh…" she looked at Brooke with pleading eyes.

I couldn't take it anymore. I saw the humiliation and pain in both Lilly's and Manda's faces. And I saw the bitterness and scorn in Brooke's sneers. All I could hear in my head was Ivy's sweet voice: "Livi, you need to follow your heart, share your truths, and dance in the rain."

I stood up from my seat and faced Brooke directly. I took a deep breath so that I would appear calm and controlled, even though I felt my blood boiling inside of me.

"You are mistaken, Brooke, if you think that Lilly made the team unfairly. You are right when you say that she didn't try out on the same day that we all did. But what you apparently don't know is that Miss Curtis had announced at the end of that day that there would be additional tryouts the next day for all those who couldn't make the tryouts that day." By now, you could have heard a pin drop on that bus. "So Lilly went the next day—all by herself, I might add—and with no help or encouragement from any one of us; she tried out with Miss Curtis. And she made the team—fair and square. And I, for one, am so incredibly proud of her!"

A sudden burst of applause exploded throughout the bus.

"Congratulations, Lilly!" popped up from all over the bus. One more time, I high-fived Lilly, and then—feeling drained— I quietly sat down. I felt relief when I noticed that Brooke had also sat down. She held her head down and was rummaging through her backpack. Manda turned and glanced at me, and when she saw that I was looking directly at her, she shot me a sheepish smile. She moved her lips and mouthed the words *thank you* to me. Then she just put her head down and looked at her hands.

Within moments, the normal bus chatter resumed. Ebony, Lilly, and I resumed talking to each other. We attempted a normal conversation, but our eyes told each other that this was definitely not a normal conversation.

At the corner of Hickory and Elm, the bus downshifted and jerked to a stop. Brooke and Manda walked down the aisle in silence, climbed down the stairs, and jumped off the bus. I watched out the window as they quickly waved good-bye to each other and then turned and began walking in opposite directions—each with her head down.

A few moments later, the bus again jolted to a stop. Ebony rose, tossed her backpack over her shoulder, and smiled at Lilly and me. "Love you guys," she said as she started down the aisle. When she got to the front of the bus, she turned and waved, and then she hopped off. With an enormous smile on her face, she waved to us as the bus jolted us forward.

"Well, this is me," Lilly said, and she stood and flung her backpack up and over her shoulders. She held onto the seat so that she wouldn't fall as the bus, once again, came to a stop. "Thank you, Livi," she whispered. "Love you!" She made her way up the aisle, stopping to let others go ahead of her. She held her head high and walked with a spring in her step. Just before she turned to go down the steps, she looked back and waved.

Lilly smiled the biggest and most brilliant smile I had ever seen her smile.

My heart was nearly exploding. I was so proud of Lilly. And I was so proud of myself for defending Lilly. And I was suddenly aware that Bobby Hendry was smiling at me. There were only a few kids left on the bus, and I heard him clearly when he said, "That was really nice of you, Livi—and brave—to clear things up for Brooke. I was about to come to Lilly's rescue, because I had actually seen her trying out with Miss Curtis that day, but you beat me to it. Lilly is lucky to have a good friend like you."

"Thanks," I said. "And, again, congrats to you, Bobby, for making the boys' team. I hadn't realized that you were trying out."

"Yeah, thanks," he answered. "Maybe someday we can run together—you know—practice." Now it was his turn to blush. "Go, Wildcats!"

"Sure," I said, and watched him go down the aisle. I watched him through the window, and I waved back to him after he waved up at me. Then I just sat back and relaxed until the bus turned into Cider Mill Road.

23

The next several days were a blur. Besides being buried in classes and homework, cross-country practices had begun. Somehow I managed to get seven hours of sleep every night. Some mornings I didn't even remember going to bed the night before. My life was busy—and I was the happiest I had been in a long time. I loved the bond that Ebony, Lilly, and I had formed, and I loved that we three shared all the activities that being on the cross-country team demanded.

It still saddened me that Brooke and Manda seemed so detached from us. In spite of everything, there were many things about each of them that I really liked. Since I had dared to challenge Brooke on the bus that day, she not only ignored me, she went out of her way to walk the other way if she saw me coming. At cross-country practices, I caught her staring and glaring at me several times, but when I tried to wave or acknowledge her, she put her chin up in the air and then whirled around. She made it quite clear that she did not consider me a friend anymore.

I wondered why I felt so bothered and troubled by it. I guess I wasn't used to having someone dislike me. I didn't know how to handle it. And I seemed unable to let it go.

Manda seemed not only distant but also sad and frightened. And I think she was probably feeling humiliated that she was still under Brooke's grip and didn't know how to get out from under it. I had tried to pull her aside between classes so that we could talk, but she refused to look at me and practically ran in the opposite direction.

I welcomed the weekend, when I could just relax and put all the drama aside. I was thrilled that the weatherman had been right in predicting that both Saturday and Sunday would be rainy with an occasional thunder-and-lightning storm. I stayed at home with Grammie and Papa, and we all lounged in our sweats for the entire weekend. We watched movies, played Scrabble, and enjoyed our laziness. It was too dark and dreary in the attic, so I avoided the Hideaway.

By the time Monday morning arrived, I was chomping at the bit, really ready to resume school. I hadn't talked to Ebony or Lilly all weekend, and I was looking forward to seeing them to catch up. Ebony and I were surprised that Lilly was not on the bus in the morning. Practice after school was uneventful. Brooke even came up to Ebony and me and made small talk. Her mood seemed somewhat lighter, and she even commented that she wondered why Lilly had not been at school. That afternoon, I went home feeling somewhat better about everything. *Maybe everything will be okay now. Maybe Brooke realizes that it is better to "make love, not war."* I slept peacefully that night.

But what I went into on Tuesday morning pretty much shattered my dream. Lilly was on the bus, sitting with Ebony; I sat down on the seat in front of them. Lilly was staring out the window and didn't look at me and didn't even acknowledge me. I looked at Ebony questioningly. Ebony's eyes were wide-opened, and she was tight-lipped. Glancing sideways toward Lilly, she subtly, but almost frantically, shook her head from side to side, signaling me to refrain from speaking to Lilly. Feeling confused, I simply sat down and pulled my math workbook from my backpack. I pretended to be deeply engrossed in completing my homework—which I had actually done as soon as I had gotten home the day before.

When we arrived at school, I took my time putting my book back into my backpack. I noticed that Ebony and Lilly were hanging back too. We were the last to step off the bus, and when I finally turned to Lilly, I gasped. I looked from Lilly to Ebony in disbelief.

"Oh my God! Lilly! What happened to you?" I said, staring at Lilly's obvious black eye. It was her right eye, and it was black and blue and swollen shut.

Lilly immediately covered her eye with her hand and began to cry. "You are not going to believe me when I tell you."

"*Tell* us, Lilly. What in the world happened?" Ebony tried to gently touch Lilly's cheek, but Lilly winced and pulled away.

Lilly told us her story. It was a very difficult story to hear. In fact, it was a tragic story. And we didn't know what to do about it.

Tuesday, October 14

Dear Ivy,

You need to help me sort this out! I don't know how to handle this! Lilly is really in trouble. And, for now, Ebony and I have promised her we won't tell a soul about what happened.

Lilly was on cloud nine a week ago on Monday when she found out that she made the team—and Ebony and I were deliriously happy for her too! It felt like a miracle that all three of us made the team! We have become such good friends, and we were so happy that we would be able to go to practices and meets together.

Of course, on the bus ride home that same Monday, Brooke had tried to crush our high spirits by accusing Lilly of making the team unfairly—right in front of everyone on the bus! I felt so bad for poor Lilly. She was so embarrassed and humiliated. You would have been proud of me if you had seen what I did— but maybe you did. Did you, Ivy? Did you see what I did? If you did, then you know that I was shaking in my boots when I set Brooke straight on that!

Brooke was obviously embarrassed when I did that, but sheesh, Ivy, she was so mean to Lilly that I couldn't just let her bad-mouth Lilly anymore. I am sad to say that Brooke doesn't handle being humiliated in public. She made Lilly pay for that, even though it was really me *she was mad at for calling her out.*

Oh, Ivy, it seems that Brooke phoned Lilly this past Friday afternoon and pretended to be sorry for what she had accused her of and for doing it in front of everyone on the bus. She asked Lilly if she could go over to her house so that they could talk. And poor gullible Lilly said okay—that "that would be nice."

Well, just as Brooke got to Lilly's house, Lilly's dad was driving off. When Lilly answered the door, Brooke pushed her way in and started poking Lilly in the chest—really hard. Lilly said Brooke pushed her up against the wall and was yelling in her face, something like, "You are such a loser, Lilly! Do you really think you stand a chance at winning against me? Your friends Livi and Ebony are crazy if they think you do! And who does Livi think she is—a new brat in town standing up and putting me down in front of everyone? Livi and Ebony are both losers, and neither one of them will ever beat me at cross-country. You're all losers! And you're the biggest loser of all, Lilly!" And, according to Lilly, that's when Brooke hauled off and punched her right in the eye. Lilly said she fell to the floor and just rolled up into a ball because Brooke started kicking her in the stomach. Poor Lilly said she couldn't even see to defend herself. She said Brooke screamed into her ear just before she left: "If you know what's good for you, Lilly, you will forget about being on the team. You are a loser, Lilly, and we don't want any losers on the team. And that goes for Livi and Ebony too. You can tell them that for me!"

So, Ivy, you see? I don't know what to do. I know that even though I promised Lilly that I wouldn't tell a soul, I must tell someone! Brooke can't be allowed to do what she did. And who knows what else she will do. Lilly has every right to be on the team. She made the team fair and square! And, Ebony and I have every right to be on the team too. The only loser I see here is Brooke. And something needs to be done to stop her. Problem is, I just don't know what that something is.

I am so sad, Ivy.

Loving you,
Livi

24

Grammie gasped. "Oh my God, Olivia!" she said. "That is just awful! We need to tell someone about this. No one should be allowed to do that—to assault someone. Did Lilly at least get checked out by a doctor? Poor little Lilly!" Grammie had tears in her eyes.

"When Lilly's father saw her later that night, she told him that she had been hit in the eye by a tennis ball at the sports complex up the road; and she said she told him that it was 'just a bruise.'" I looked over at Papa and then at Grammie. "Lilly doesn't even play tennis. I don't think her dad has a clue about what Lilly does and doesn't do. Lilly's mom died of cancer a few years back, and it seems like Lilly spends most of her time alone. Lilly said that even when her dad *is* home, he seems totally out of the picture."

"Oh, that poor little girl. She must be so lonely. It is bad enough that she lost her mom but to have pretty much lost her dad too…well, that is just unthinkable."

At the same moment, Grammie, Papa, and I realized the irony of those words. Grammie reached over and hugged me. "Oh, Livi—at least we have each other. There is no way we could have gotten this far without the love and support of each other. Poor little Lilly has no one—except for you and Ebony."

"So, what should we do?" I asked. "What should *I* do? I know we have to do *something*! Lilly was in school yesterday, but she was absent again today, and I am really worried that something is terribly wrong!"

"Well," Papa said, shaking his head, "I think the first thing we need to do is let Lilly's dad know what really happened so that he can make sure she gets medical care—to make sure Lilly doesn't have any broken bones and to make sure no permanent damage was done to her eye or any of her internal organs." Papa continued to shake his head. "This is really a serious matter."

"And then," Grammie added, "this needs to be reported to the school principal. This was a serious assault. And this was a very serious breach of moral conduct." Grammie closed her eyes. "I can't believe that this has happened. I know one thing, we have to help Lilly in any way we can. She can't get through this on her own. Poor little Lilly...poor little Lilly."

We sat in silence around the kitchen table, engrossed in our own thoughts. The sudden jangle of the phone made us jump.

It was kind of eerie when I heard Lilly's voice. "Hi, Liv," she said softly. "Can you talk?"

Wide-eyed, I motioned to Grammie and Papa that it was Lilly on the phone. "What should I say?" I whispered to them as I held the phone tight against my chest.

Gram whispered back, "Just hear what she has to say. Just listen. We'll figure something out. Let her know we are here for her—whatever it takes."

I nodded and ran up the stairs two at a time. I sat in my rocking chair and did what Grammie suggested. I just listened.

Lilly continued to speak softly and all in one tone. She sounded sad, lonely, and somber. She was home alone. It was just after dinnertime on Wednesday, and she explained why she had not been at school all day. She said she had had an awful headache, along with sharp pains in her chest and stomach. She said her eye still felt uncomfortable but that the swelling had gone down quite a bit. She also said that she was afraid to go to school because she was afraid of Brooke.

I could not "just listen" anymore. I told Lilly that I had told Grammie and Papa what had happened to her. And I told her that Grammie and Papa said that we would stand by her and help her through this. I told her that Grammie and Papa felt it was very important that they speak to her dad and that this whole mess must be reported to the authorities. I told her everything.

I was expecting some sort of protest from Lilly.

But all Lilly said was, "Okay, Livi. I know you are right. Thanks."

The next day was Thursday, and it started out like any other day—except that Lilly was not on the bus again. So I knew I would not see her at practice. What I didn't know was that all hell was breaking loose.

Ebony and I had kept Lilly's secret at school. We both knew it was very important to keep this a private matter, because matters like this, when leaked, became a source entertainment to all those who aren't involved. And that was the last thing that Lilly needed.

When Gram picked me up after practice, she was very serious and anxious. On the ride home, she told me that she and Papa had gone, unannounced, to visit Lilly's dad.

"He was shocked when he heard what had happened. But he also was very concerned, and he wrapped his arms around Lilly and hugged her for a long time. He told her he was so sorry that he hadn't been there for her since her mom had died." Gram had tears in her eyes when she said, "He apologized to Lilly for 'letting her down.' He broke down and cried his heart out, and then it was Lilly who hugged him tightly for a long time."

Gram went on to say that, while she and Papa were still there, Lilly's dad had called and made an appointment with the doctor for later that afternoon. He promised that he would phone Grammie and Papa when he got home to let them know how Lilly was doing. He also said that he realized it was sadly necessary to report the incident to the school authorities.

"It was strange, Livi," Gram said. "As bad as all that was, it somehow seemed to bring Lilly and her dad closer together. I saw a lot of love in that room."

I was so grateful to Grammie and Papa for doing what they did. I knew it must have been really hard to do. I longed to talk to Lilly, but Gram said I should try to give her some space right now. So that's what I did. Later that evening, I called Ebony and shared Lilly's story with her. She, too, seemed relieved that Lilly's problem was being dealt with. For the first time, Ebony and I were at a loss for words. We both felt sad but relieved. All we could do was wait to see how it all played out. We hung up but not before we said "I love you" to each other.

I prayed to Mom and Dad and Ivy that night before I fell asleep. *Please make this all better, for everyone's sake—especially for Lilly's. I'm so afraid that this will never be over, that it will never be made right.*

The last thing I heard in my head before drifting off to sleep was Dad's deep voice: "Never say never, Olivia."

25

While having breakfast Friday morning, Grammie told me that Lilly's dad had kept his promise and had called the night before. She said his call had come almost at midnight. He said he and Lilly had just returned home after spending the entire evening at the emergency room. Dr. McGrath had examined Lilly in his office but then sent them to the hospital so that Lilly could have an eye exam, X-rays and CAT scans, and blood work to determine if she had received any damage to bones or body organs. The doctor told Lilly's dad that she was very lucky, because other than the severe bruises she had received from the assault, everything else appeared to be normal.

Grammie said that Lilly's dad had sounded exhausted but relieved as he told her the results. He also told Grammie that the doctor had given him a written report of the findings—that the injuries were consistent with Lilly's claims of being assaulted.

Grammie said that Lilly and her dad were going to the school in the morning to make an official report of the assault that Brooke had inflicted on Lilly. He wasn't sure what would happen after that, but Grammie gave him permission to give my name if the authorities needed to talk to me. Lilly's dad had also called Ebony's mom and dad, who also gave permission to give Ebony's name.

Suddenly this all seemed so much more serious than before—and very official. I felt sad that Lilly had to go through all this. She had been so happy and proud of herself only six days ago. She had been so enthusiastic and cheerful— even bubbly—after learning she had made the team. It just seemed as though poor Lilly could never catch a break. And I was feeling guilty, because I was the one who had pushed her to try out for the team. If I had just minded my own business, if I had just kept my mouth shut on the bus and not challenged Brooke—maybe none of this would have happened, or maybe I would have been the one Brooke targeted, instead of Lilly.

Grammie warned me that there was a possibility that both Ebony and I might be called into the meeting during the day, but she assured me that if that were to happen, she and Papa would insist that they be present. And she assumed that Ebony's mom and dad would do the same.

"If it happens that you get called in, Livi, you have an easy part in all of this: just tell the truth as you know it."

Ebony and I never spoke about any of it on the bus. We both knew how important it was for us to keep this to ourselves. Once we got to school, we hugged good-bye, and it was then that I whispered in Ebony's ear, "Maybe I'll see you if we get called to Lilly's meeting."

Ebony, tight-lipped, shrugged her shoulders. "I love you, Livs," she whispered as she turned to head to class.

I nodded, "Love you, too, Ebs."

All through the morning, all through lunch, my stomach was tied up in knots. I became nauseous when Brooke and Manda sat down with Ebony and me in the cafeteria. Brooke was more talkative than usual, more cheerful than usual, and very interested in why Lilly hadn't been in school the last few days. Manda, on the other hand, sat sullen and made no eye contact and no conversation.

Brooke finally came right out and asked me if I knew why Lilly hadn't been in school. I couldn't tell a lie—a lie is a lie is a lie—so I just shrugged my shoulders and said nothing. Ebony faked having to go to the bathroom and never returned. When the bell rang, signaling that our lunch period was almost over, I jumped up.

"I've got to run," I said. "I have an assignment to make up." I glanced over at Manda who continued to sit with her head down. I noticed a tear running down her cheek. When I glanced at Brooke, I saw a smug look on her face.

"See you at practice!" she beamed as she picked up her tray and prepared to leave. "Are you coming, Manda?" she asked.

"Uh, no," Manda answered, "I'm not done eating."

Brooke gave Manda a questioning look. "Suit yourself. What'd you do, get up on the wrong side of the bed this morning?" With that, Brooke turned and fell into step beside me.

"You and Ebony are kind of quiet today. What's up?" Brooke said, and stepped in front of me so that I had to stop.

I avoided looking directly at Brooke. "I really have to run," I said. "I've got that assignment to make up before math class starts. See ya." I stepped around Brooke and broke out into a slow run.

I heard Brooke say, "Okay, then—I'll see you in math class!"

It was just five minutes until the bell would ring for the start of math class. I plopped down into my seat, exhausted from all of the mental stress over the last four days. Mr. Tauro nonchalantly walked up to me and handed me a note.

"If you don't make it back in time," he said, "you can take the quiz during your next free period."

I quickly read the note: *Olivia Breton, please report at once to Counselor Seybolt's office in the administration building.*

I practically crashed into Brooke as I was exiting the classroom. "Oops, sorry," I said, offering no explanation as to why I was leaving class.

Brooke's expression was one of confusion. "What the hell?" she said under her breath. "Where are you going?"

I pretended I hadn't heard her, and I rounded the bannister and flew down the stairs. I felt like my heart was going to explode. Once outside, the cold autumn air felt good against my face. I slowed my pace and tried to catch my breath. I had a pain in my stomach, and I was afraid I was going to throw up. I forced myself to breathe slowly. *Calm down*, I told myself. *All you have to do is tell the truth.*

By the time I opened the ornately carved door of the administration building, I could hear my heartbeat pounding in my ears. My hands shook as I handed my note to the receptionist at the desk.

"Hi, Olivia," she smiled. "Mrs. Seybolt's office is down that hall, last door on the left. Just knock on the door."

As soon as I knocked, the door opened. Mrs. Seybolt—who I had never even set eyes on before—smiled and motioned for me to enter. "Come on in. You must be Olivia?"

"Yes," I tried to say. Suddenly my throat and mouth were parched. I coughed.

"Why don't you get yourself a bottle of water," Mrs. Seybolt pointed to the refrigerator across the room. "Anyone else want some water?"

It was then that I noticed that I was not the only one in the room. Seated around a large conference table were Grammie and Papa, Ebony's mom and dad, and Ebony. Mrs. Seybolt directed me to find a seat. Papa motioned to the empty chair between Grammie and him. Once I was settled, I looked across the table and smiled at Ebony and her mom and dad. I had never met them before, but it was clear that Ebony was their daughter. The resemblance between Ebony and her mom was striking. And she had inherited her beautiful smile and perfect teeth from her dad.

"Well, we finally meet," Ebony's mom said softly. Her smile warmed my heart.

"How do you do, Livi?" her dad nodded and smiled.

Mrs. Seybolt was slender and stood at least six feet in height—a tall drink of water, Dad would have said. She was more handsome than pretty and had a pleasant inviting smile. She removed her glasses from her pointy nose and placed them on top of her head as she made her way to her seat at the head of the conference table.

"Okay," she said. "So it seems everyone here has introduced themselves." She smiled and slowly looked around the table. "Let me formally introduce myself. I am Shirley Seybolt—safe-school-climate specialist and counselor. I have called you all here today so that we can talk about a very serious matter—a matter that could potentially threaten the safety of all in this room. Before we start, I need to stress that everything that is said in this room must be kept confidential. We can only continue here if I have everyone's signature agreeing to that. Please turn over the form that is in front of you, and, if you agree to this, please sign the form and pass it back to me."

The room was silent except for the faint sound of music coming from somewhere near Counselor Seybolt's desk. I was sure the music was supposed to relax us, and now that I was aware of it, I actually did feel a little more at ease.

The forms were signed and passed back. We all watched as Mrs. Seybolt looked over each form. "Okay, great," she said, and smiled and set the papers down on the table. She looked around the table at each one of us. "Let me start by saying how proud I am of both Olivia and Ebony for their willingness to take part in this investigation. I know this is pretty scary. And I know you must have many concerns. I want you to know that I recognize the courage it requires to do what you are doing. But the bottom line is this: it is the right thing to do."

"And," she continued, "to the parents and guardians here in this room, I want to thank you for supporting these two young ladies."

Counselor Seybolt went on to explain how the process worked. She referred to Lilly as the person "who initiated the complaint." She explained that she had this person's written report of the incident. She explained that she would speak individually to me first, with Grammie and Papa present, and then to Ebony with her parents present. Ebony and I would each then have to submit a written report of everything that we knew that we felt was in anyway related to the incident—whether it had happened before the actual incident, during the incident, or after the incident. She said it didn't matter if it had happened on school grounds, on a school bus, at an off-campus function, or at any other place. It was her job to do an extensive investigation to determine if there was any act that had the potential of disrupting a student's—any student's—education, or that had the potential of disrupting the orderly operation of the school.

Counselor Seybolt looked from me to Ebony and then from Grammie and Papa to Ebony's parents. She looked down at her hands for just a moment. Then she said, "I will then meet privately with the person—in the presence of her parents—against whom the original complaint has been filed. She will be required to submit a written report also. I will then review all the written reports, and I will consider all the information I have gathered from talking to each and every one of you. If, after I review all that, I determine that this has been an act of bullying, I will recommend a plan of intervention with all those involved. If I determine that it is necessary, I will recommend disciplinary action. I will keep our principal, Mr. Pffeifer, informed of every step along the way. If he determines that the act of bullying constitutes criminal conduct, he must report the matter to the police.

You could have heard a pin drop in that room. The seriousness of this was driven home to us when the words "act of bullying" and "criminal conduct" were spoken. The air seemed heavy with the weight of the burden that had been placed on each of us.

The faint sound of music had become annoying and was giving me a headache. I put my hands over my eyes and fought against the tears that were threatening to spill out any second. I took a deep breath.

"Are you okay, Olivia?" Mrs. Seybolt asked. "Should we take a short break?"

Once Papa put his arm around my back, I seemed to relax some.

"No, I'm okay," I said. I was losing my voice again. I took a quick swig of water. "I'm okay," I said again. My voice had returned.

"How are you doing, Ebony?" Mrs. Seybolt asked. "Do you need a break?"

"No, I'm okay. This is just so upsetting and scary," Ebony said softly. Her voice was shaking.

"Very well, then," Mrs. Seybolt said. "If it's okay with you, Olivia, I'd like to ask you and your grandparents to come with me to another private office. While we are talking and getting your written report in there, I'd like to offer some refreshments to the rest of you. Please stretch your legs, use the restrooms, and get comfortable on the sofas. All I ask is that you refrain from talking about the incident."

As we were leaving this room, the nice receptionist who had spoken to me earlier was delivering a large platter of pastries and fruit. Behind her, another woman rolled in a cart with beverages.

I glanced back into the room and saw Ebony leaning into her dad. She looked down at the floor and her shoulders slumped. I knew exactly how she felt.

26

Unlike the huge conference room, the room we moved to was a much smaller room with only a small table and four chairs in the center. And, thank God, there was no music. Mrs. Seybolt, Grammie, Papa, and I got comfortable. It was unusually warm for October 20, and a refreshing breeze blew in through a half-opened window directly behind me.

"Okay, let's get started," Mrs. Seybolt said as she slid a short stack of paper forms to me across the table. "First of all, let me define again what determines *bullying*. Based on a Connecticut law, bullying can include a variety of behaviors, but all involve individuals or a group who are trying to take advantage of the power they have to hurt or reject others. These behaviors can be carried out physically by hitting, kicking, pushing, and so forth; verbally by calling names, threatening, teasing, taunting, or spreading rumors; or in other ways, such as leaving them out of activities, not talking to them, stealing or damaging their things, making them feel uncomfortable and scared, or making faces or obscene gestures."

I was sitting on my hands and staring at the turquoise glass vase of orange and yellow flowers that sat in the center of the table. There were two small pumpkins that sat on either side of it. My mind wandered to last Halloween. I jumped when Mrs. Seybolt spoke my name.

"Are you with me, Olivia?" she smiled. "I know this must be very uncomfortable and scary for you, but I need you to read the instructions on the statement form and then write a full account of everything you remember that has anything to do with what led up to the incident that we have been addressing today. Please don't leave anything out, even if you think it might not be important or crucial to this matter. Please include all that pertains to this matter, whether it is something that happened to someone else or to you. I have given you plenty of paper and a guideline to follow."

Mrs. Seybolt turned to Grammie and then to Papa. "I am going to ask you both to step out while Olivia writes her statement. You will have a chance to look over her statement before she submits it to me to be sure you are comfortable with it." Then, turning back to me, she said, "And remember, Olivia, all you need to do is tell the truth—this will be kept strictly confidential and will only be used in determining what, if anything, will be done to handle this situation."

Grammie and Papa each gave me a hug and then quietly left the room. Mrs. Seybolt placed a bottle of water near me on the table. "Take your time, Olivia." As she turned to leave, she looked back and said, "I am very proud of you for taking part in this. Just tell the truth. There are no right answers, and there are no wrong answers. When you are done, just go to the sitting area and tell your grandparents. They may then go back into the conference room with you and look over your statement. They can discuss any concerns they might have with you at that time. Once you are all satisfied with the statement, please go to the receptionist and tell her you are ready to submit it, and I will come to you to get it."

As soon as the door was closed and I was alone, I began to cry. I didn't know where to begin, so I began at the beginning.

I wrote of how I had first met Brooke: of how, on several occasions, Brooke had come to my rescue; that she had seemed to be taking me under her wing. I wrote about the red flags I had sensed at the sleepover: how Brooke had conned me into joining her to prank Manda and Lilly by yelling *Boo!* as they approached and how she had turned it around on me, claiming it had been my idea, and then acted as though she were mad at me for doing it. I wrote about how Brooke frequently played Manda and Lilly against each other and about how distressed Lilly had become over that kind of behavior. I wrote about how I sensed that Manda was feeling increasingly controlled by Brooke, how she was almost forced to be mean to both Lilly and me for fear of being unwanted, rejected, and shut out by Brooke. I described how sad, tearful, and ashamed Manda had appeared that day on the school bus after Brooke had humiliated Lilly about making the cross-country team "unfairly" and how Manda had turned to me and mouthed "thank you" to me after I had stood up for Lilly. I wrote about how I had noticed recently that Manda seemed increasingly more quiet, sullen, and detached from everyone, even Brooke.

I sat and stared at the paper as my mind drifted to that day in the bathroom at school—that day when I overheard Brooke talking to Manda and a few other girls who I didn't know.

I wasn't sure that I should include that in my statement, but then I remembered Mrs. Seybolt's instructions: *include everything and anything you remember that pertains to this situation, whether or not you feel it is crucial to this matter.* So I continued to write: about how Brooke had laughed when she told the others that I thought I could make the cross-country team, about how she "had news for me." I wrote about how she said I was a snot and how I thought I was better than everyone else because I had gone to a hoity-toity school in Cape Cod.

I wrote about how Brooke's intimidation of Lilly seemed to increase after Lilly and I were getting closer and developing a friendship. I wrote about how Lilly had phoned me one evening—about how she had been crying and about how she asked me if she could talk to me. I wrote about how Ebony, who was there with me, suggested we invite Lilly over so that we could talk. I wrote about Ebony's strength and good character and about how we had become such good friends. I wrote about how supportive Ebony and I had been when Lilly had come over to my house that night and how, after that night, we three had become good friends. I wrote about how I had noticed that since we had become friends, Brooke's shunning of both Lilly and me had become worse.

I wrote and wrote and wrote until I began to get spasms in my back and cramps in my hand. I put the pen down, sat up straight in my chair, and stretched out my hand and fingers. I twisted the cap off the bottle of water that Mrs. Seybolt had placed next to me earlier and took a few sips. I took a deep breath, picked up my pen, bent over my statement, and began to write again.

I wrote about how Lilly had shared with me her story of being bullied at her previous school; how she had devised a plan to outrun the bullies; and how, in doing so, she had become such a fast runner. I wrote about how I had encouraged Lilly to put her speed to good use. I wrote about how guilty I felt—how responsible I felt—for pushing Lilly to try out for the cross-country team, even though Lilly told me she "just couldn't do that." I wrote about how proud I was of Lilly when I learned that she had, on her own, gone to the second day of tryouts and how proud of Lilly I was when I learned that she had made the team.

I wrote about how guilty I felt for setting Brooke straight—challenging her—on the school bus that day after Brooke had, in front of everyone on the bus, humiliated Lilly by saying that Lilly had made the team unfairly and that Lilly hadn't even tried out like the rest of us.

I wrote about how bad I felt that, because I had dared to challenge Brooke in front of the entire bus, she was mad at me and was taking out her anger on Lilly. I wrote about Lilly's account of how Brooke had gone to her house and beat her up. I wrote that Lilly had told me that Brooke had told her, "If you know what's good for you, Lilly, you'll forget about being on the team." I wrote that Lilly had told me that Brooke had also told Lilly she was a loser, that "Ebony and Livi were losers too," and that "no one wanted losers on the team." I wrote that Lilly told me Brooke had said, "And you can tell Ebony and Livi that for me." I wrote about how humiliated and upset Lilly seemed after that incident.

That was it. I couldn't write another word. I didn't even re-read my statement. I had told the truth as I knew it. And that was all I could do.

27

It was almost five o'clock when Grammie, Papa, and I left the meeting at the school. Once in the car, I couldn't hold the tears back anymore. I started to sob and couldn't stop. Grammie and Papa tried giving me words of support and encouragement, but all I could do was blubber. Grammie finally told me to just let it out.

"For all you've been through, Livi," she said from the front seat, "I think you deserve a good cry." And that's just what I did for the next ten minutes. Once I had "permission" to cry, I let loose. My chest jerked in spasms; I wept loudly at first, and then, finally, my sobs were reduced to soft whimpers.

The mood in the car was solemn. A heaviness seemed to hang in the air. Papa's words sliced through the gloom and broke the spell: "Anyone up for ice cream?"

All at once, we exploded into laughter. My chest heaved as I tried to catch my breath. I dabbed my eyes, snorted, and blew my nose—and noticed that Grammie was doing the same.

Once I could breathe again, my eyes drifted toward Papa's rearview mirror, and I realized that he was looking at me too.

"Whew!" Papa said, and laughed. "You and your grandmother are a sight! Give me your orders, and I'll go in and get it. You two stay right there."

While we waited, Grammie and I sat in silence, obviously immersed in our own thoughts. As I stared unconsciously at the big red *Friendly's Ice Cream* sign, I felt relieved, lighter, cleansed, and full of hope. I wasn't sure how this would turn out, but I had faith that somehow it would all be resolved, and the outcome would be good. But I also feared that I might be feeling too optimistic. I finally realized that I was way too weary to spend any energy on thinking. I made a conscious decision to avoid thinking about anything for the rest of the evening—other than the sundae Papa was carrying back to the car.

I don't know if I have ever enjoyed a sundae—chocolate ice cream with hot fudge, whipped cream, walnuts, and a cherry—as much as I did during that ride home. I stayed true to my decision. I kept my mind free of unpleasant thoughts. I focused only on the treat I had in front of me. I didn't even worry about the river of hot fudge that was winding its way down my brand-new, white, Abercrombie & Fitch sweatshirt.

28

I spent a quiet weekend, and Monday morning arrived much too quickly, and it was back to the real world. I had barely sat down in my first class of the day when Mrs. Kneeland approached me.

"Olivia, you need to report to Counselor's Seybolt's office at once; do you know where it is?"

I rolled my eyes at her, took in a deep breath, and blew it out. "I know where it is."

"You should take all your things," Mrs. Kneeland smiled, "just in case you don't make it back here before class ends." As an afterthought, she whispered, "Don't worry; I'm sure you are not in any trouble."

"Thanks," I whispered back. I knew I wasn't in any trouble, but I also knew that whatever was in store for me wasn't going to be any fun.

I walked slowly to the administration building, which was on the opposite end of the college-like campus. I took deep breaths, trying to let the cold October air relax my nerves—which seemed to be on high alert. I tried to focus on the beautiful architecture of the many old buildings that made up this unique middle school and of the miles of stone walls that surrounded it. Hundreds of century-old maple trees dotted the grounds, and autumn had transformed the landscape into a backdrop of vibrant colors, making it look like a prize-winning painting.

I entered the building and stopped at the receptionist's desk. The same nice woman who I had spoken with on Friday was on the phone, but she smiled and pointed for me to go down the hall.

Mrs. Seybolt's door was ajar, but I knocked on it anyway. "Come on in," she called from inside.

Once inside, I was relieved to see Ebony and Lilly sitting together on the sofa. They were quietly speaking to each other, and when they saw me, their smiles told me they were happy to see me. I plopped down onto the sofa too. Before I had a chance to say even one word, Mrs. Seybolt joined us. She settled down into one of the two faded red leather chairs that were directly across from the sofa where the three of us sat. The leather squeaked and crackled as she adjusted her long legs; for some crazy reason—nerves, I guessed—I found that extremely funny, and I fought to stifle a giggle.

"Hi, girls," Counselor Seybolt smiled. "We are waiting for one more person, and then we'll begin. Help yourselves to some cookies and juice."

I scanned the tray of chocolate chip cookies on the coffee table before us. They looked delicious, but my stomach was doing flip-flops, so I steered clear of them. Ebony and Lilly did too. I wondered who we were waiting for. Mr. Pffeifer, the principal? Some other counselor?

There was a faint tap on the door. "Come on in," Mrs. Seybolt called.

When Manda walked in, she looked pale and frightened—and very surprised to see Ebony, Lilly, and me sitting there. We three looked wide-eyed at each other—and then at Manda and then at Mrs. Seybolt.

Mrs. Seybolt spoke first. "Have a seat, Manda," she said. She pointed to the other worn red leather chair opposite us. The room had become silent.

Manda timidly sank down into the chair. Again, the squeaking and crackling sounds of the leather struck me funny, and, again, I desperately fought to contain a giggle. I was relieved when Mrs. Seybolt began speaking.

"Let me start by saying that I have permission from your parents and, in your case, Olivia, from your grandparents, to meet with you today." Mrs. Seybolt took a sip of water from her plastic Chelsea Middle School cup. "I've asked Manda to join our group this morning. After I read all of your statements, I realized that it was important that I speak with Manda, because it was clear to me that she was, as are each of you, involved in some way in this unfortunate incident—the incident that has brought us here today. Manda has given me a written statement, just as you three ladies have."

"Let me just say again," Mrs. Seybolt said as she looked at each of us, one by one, "I am very proud of you—Lilly, Ebony, Olivia, and Manda—for having the courage to do what you have done in an effort to resolve this situation. And I want to reassure you—each of you—that there will *not* be any retaliation toward you as a result of this. If you feel in any way that you have been retaliated against for coming forward, you need to see me immediately, and I will deal with it promptly. I want you each to feel safe in every way as we move through this process."

Mrs. Seybolt slowly looked at each one of us. We each nodded. My heart was pounding, and my stomach was doing flip-flops again.

"Okay, that being said, I want to let you know where we are with all of this. I have met with our principal, Mr. Pffeifer, and filled him in on the situation. He is also very proud of you girls for coming forward. I have met with Brooke and her parents, and they have each assured me that they are willing to cooperate with our investigation and with our intervention plans. Brooke and her parents have agreed that it is in everyone's best interest that, for now, Brooke be suspended from school and school activities. I want to remind you that everything—*everything*—that is said in this room must be considered strictly confidential. That is the only fair way to handle this."

We all nodded. For the first time since the meeting had started, I made eye contact with Manda. Her lips were sealed tightly, and her eyes were brimming with tears. I sensed the pain she was going through. I smiled in an attempt to let her know I understood. In response to my smile, Manda's tears spilled out of her eyes, down her cheeks, and onto her pink sweater. She plucked a tissue out of the box that sat next to the chocolate chip cookies. She dabbed at her eyes and wiped her runny nose.

Aware that all eyes were upon her, Manda lost all restraint. She sobbed into her hands. In between breaths, her voice was deep and raspy as she choked out, "I am…so sorry. I am just… so sorry." Her chest heaving, she looked across at us.

"Oh, Manda!" I said, the first one to speak. "I know. I know how hard this is—for all of us." I lost the fight I had been having all morning. I gratefully let my tears run down my cheeks. I didn't even bother to hide them or wipe them away.

Lilly put her head down and sobbed into her hands. Her shoulders rose and fell with each sob. She tried to speak but only made squeaking noises and soon gave up.

Ebony put her arm around Lilly, and Lilly rested her head on Ebony's chest. Ebony's eyes were brimming with tears too.

I looked to Mrs. Seybolt for some guidance, for some wise solution to our outbursts, for some reassurance that we all weren't going crazy. But I saw tears in her eyes too. And I saw tolerance and love and pride. She nodded her head up and down, up and down. She let us cry out all the tension and fear, the guilt and humiliation, and the sadness and regret.

Once we had regained our composures, Mrs. Seybolt smiled and said, "Okay, now that we have that out of our systems, let's continue."

We coughed, cleared our throats, repositioned ourselves, and nodded in agreement. We breathed a collective sigh. We were ready to go on.

"Do any of you have any questions for me? Concerns? Feelings you would like to share?" Mrs. Seybolt asked. We were all quiet, lost in our own thoughts. "Lilly?" she interrupted. "What are you feeling about all this? You've been through quite an ordeal."

Lilly burst out, "I am so scared! I am scared that Brooke will beat me up again. She must be really mad at me for telling on her and for getting the school involved—and for getting her suspended. I am really just so scared of what will happen!"

"Well, first of all, Lilly, I totally understand your fears, but I must reassure you that you did the right thing by coming forward. Bullying is not acceptable—in any shape or form. And secondly, *you* did not get Brooke suspended. *Brooke* got Brooke suspended. Her actions were totally unacceptable, and that is what resulted in her suspension."

"But," Mrs. Seybolt continued, "I want to reassure you that I will—and the school will—do everything necessary to protect you from any retaliation from Brooke, or from anyone else for that matter. I hope you can believe me when I tell you this."

Lilly looked intently at Mrs. Seybolt. She nodded and smiled and took a deep breath. When it was clear that Lilly had no more to say, Mrs. Seybolt looked over at Manda.

"Manda?"

Manda also looked directly at Mrs. Seybolt. "I just want to do what is right," she said. "I really like Lilly and Ebony and Livi, and I am so sorry that I hurt them, especially Lilly. Lilly and I used to be so close...until Brooke..." She let her sentence go unfinished, but she looked across the table at Lilly. Lilly smiled sadly at Manda, nodded, and then looked away.

"Ebony?" Mrs. Seybolt looked over at Ebony, who was staring at the floor. "Do you have anything you want to say?"

"Well," Ebony began, "all I want to say is that I can understand a little of what Lilly and Manda have been through. I was bullied a little when I first moved here to Chelsea and started fifth grade. I tried to be nice to everyone, but there were a few girls—and Brooke was one of them—who were just so mean. They called me fat...and ugly...and just seemed to make a point of ignoring me. It hurt really bad.

"But I decided I had to just worry about myself. So I joined the cross-country team and found out I really liked running. Most of the girls on the team were really nice to me. And it seemed that the longer I was on the team, the more confidence I started to have in myself. No one seemed interested in bullying me anymore—maybe because they knew that I didn't let it bother me."

Ebony turned to her right to look directly at Lilly. "So, Lilly," she said, and then looked across at Manda, "and Manda, if you could try not to let it show that your feelings are hurt when someone says something to bad-mouth you, to demean you... if you could just ignore them and go about your business...they might just get tired of bullying you and move onto someone or something else." Ebony caught her breath, shrugged her shoulders, and looked down at her hands that were balled up into tight fists on her lap. "I don't know...it worked for me."

I watched as a single teardrop fell onto one of Ebony's fists. It slowly trickled down the side of her hand and disappeared.

"This is all so sad," I said, still staring at Ebony's fist. "It just seems like everything has exploded beyond recognition—like it's the end of the world—like there's no going back to when it was so easy to just play, to just be a kid. I don't understand how it got to this point. I don't understand it—and I surely don't like it." I looked up and saw everyone—even Mrs. Seybolt—nodding in agreement. "And," I continued, "crazy as it sounds, I feel sorry for Brooke." I looked around the room to see if I had upset anyone. I saw only blank expressions, so I went on. "Even though she has been so mean in so many ways, especially to Lilly, she *can* be very nice. She can be very friendly, and she can be very funny. When I went to her sleepover with Manda and Lilly, Brooke seemed to really *like it* that Manda and Lilly were being so nice to me. I really felt it was important to Brooke to make me feel welcome, to make me feel like I was accepted into their circle of friends. That was so important to me at that time, because I had just moved here, and I had left all my friends behind in Sutcliffe—I had just lost my whole family, and I was feeling so alone."

I stopped. I could feel my eyes welling up. I was so tired of crying. I looked up at the ceiling. *Keep it together*, I thought to myself. I heard Ivy's words in my head: *You can do this, Livi.* I took a deep breath, puffed up my cheeks, and blew it out.

"What I am trying to say is, yes, Brooke has some serious problems. I don't know why, but she seems jealous of us, of Manda, Ebony, me, and especially Lilly. And I don't understand *that*, because she seems to have everything going for her, but why else would she bad-mouth us, try to control who we can be friends with, and try to keep Ebony, Lilly and me from running on the cross-country team? She just must be so unhappy with herself. I really do feel sorry for her—even after all she has done."

"I don't understand it either, Livi," Lilly said softly. She shook her head back and forth. "I don't understand it; I just wanted to be her friend."

"Why would she be jealous of *us*?" Manda said, gawking at me in disbelief.

I shrugged my shoulders; I was beginning to regret that I had spoken up about it. I looked to Mrs. Seybolt to rescue me.

"Well," Mrs. Seybolt began, "I believe that, indeed, Brooke *is* jealous of each and every one of you—because, despite all Brooke may have, she wants to be you. She obviously sees something in each one of you that she wishes she had, and I am not talking about money or possessions. I believe Brooke sees qualities in each of your characters that she wishes she had too. I don't believe she is even aware of that, but I do believe that it is what has propelled Brooke to act out the way she has."

"And, yes, Olivia," Mrs. Seybolt looked directly across at me, "this is all so sad. Indeed, this is all so sad."

"So, how do we fix this?" I asked. It was my turn to look directly across at Mrs. Seybolt. "It's one thing to keep us safe from Brooke, but how do we *fix this*, Mrs. Seybolt?" I could hear my voice getting louder and louder. "How do *we* fix this? How do we help Brooke feel better about her own self, so that she doesn't need to hurt us just so she can feel better about herself?" I'm not sure why, but I was feeling more angry by the second. "How do we fix this, Mrs. Seybolt?"

I was relieved when Ebony broke in. "I agree," she said. "It doesn't seem good enough to just keep us safe. I mean, yes, that is really important to all of us, but it seems important to help Brooke too." Ebony looked around at each of us and then directly at Mrs. Seybolt. "I mean, Brooke must be hurting too. She must feel humiliated and ashamed of what she has done, of how she has treated all of us. And, I agree with Livi—Brooke can be nice when she wants to be. It must be sad to be Brooke."

Ebony turned and put her hand on Lilly's shoulder. "I hope you are not mad at me for saying this, Lilly, but I must admit that I feel sorry for Brooke too."

"I never looked at it like that before," Lilly said, her voice shaking. "I guess I never realized that maybe Brooke needs us more than we need her."

Manda stared at the floor. She nodded her head in agreement. "I guess you may be right, Lilly," she said. "Boy! I never thought we'd be saying *that!*"

We each looked at one another in obvious amazement. We remained silent and perfectly still until Mrs. Seybolt's words broke the spell.

"So, you asked me what we can do to fix all of this," she said. Mrs. Seybolt was quiet for a moment. "Well, I am blown away by you girls. I am blown away by your sensitivity, by your wisdom, and by your desire to resolve this matter, not just for your own benefits, but for Brooke's benefit too. That really would be a win-win situation."

Mrs. Seybolt crossed her hands on her lap and continued. "How would you feel about meeting as a group with Brooke? Here in the privacy of my office, where I can supervise and make sure that things don't get out of hand."

We each looked from one to the other. We all were wide-eyed, tight-lipped, and flabbergasted. I saw that Lilly, Ebony, and Manda were as stunned as I was. We hadn't expected that! What had I started here? I had said I wished we could help Brooke, but I never dreamed that we would have to meet with her.

"Do you think that will work?" I asked Mrs. Seybolt, still stunned.

"Well," Mrs. Seybolt answered calmly, "it might. It certainly is something to think about. If you girls could open up to Brooke in the kind and sensitive way you opened up to me today, well, yes, it might just work." She slowly looked at each of us. "What do you think?"

"Wow," was all I could say. I looked to Ebony, Lilly, and Manda for some kind of sentiment.

Ebony spoke first. "I'm okay with that, but I think Lilly is the one who has to be okay with that." Ebony turned to Lilly. "Lilly, would you be okay with that? I'd understand if you wouldn't feel safe with that after what Brooke did to you."

Lilly's eyes were closed. When she opened her eyes, they seemed bright and clear and determined. "I can't believe I am saying this, but, yes, I would be okay with that. The way I see it, things right now are as bad as they can be. And if meeting here with Brooke might help make things better—maybe even make things good—then I say *let's go for it*." Lilly's jaw was set, and her next words were deliberate: "I sure don't want to spend every minute looking over my shoulder, being afraid that Brooke is going to pop out and beat me up again."

Lilly's face became soft; her eyes were warm and gentle, pale and blue—like forget-me-nots in a spring bouquet—and she seemed at peace. "I would rather us be at peace than at war. I say, let's go for it. What do we have to lose?"

29

Saturday, October 26

Dear Ivy,

I am so glad it is Saturday, and I don't have to go to school for two whole days. My life has been so incredibly crazy these last few weeks! I don't know where to begin.

The first two meetings with Mrs. Seybolt were really un-comfortable and scary, but I guess I'd have to say that they really helped to give us a chance to get so much off our chests. The bottom line is this: It is not *okay for Brooke to bully us! It is* not *okay for anyone to bully anyone! And it is* not *okay to beat anyone up!*

But there is so much more to this, Ivy. Poor Lilly is the one who got beat up, and she was sure upset about it—but I was really upset too by all the drama and the hurt and the waking up to how wacky and cruel this world can really be. I never realized that people could be so mean or so twisted or so mis-understood. I guess we—you and I—were really lucky to have Mom and Dad as our parents. We just always knew we were loved. I guess it was stupid of me to assume all of my friends felt that their parents loved them too.

The third meeting we had this past Tuesday was with Brooke—in Mrs. Seybolt's office. It was kind of weird because a school security officer stood outside the door in case the meeting got out of hand. The meeting was scary at first. I was so nervous; I thought I was going to throw up—then I thought I was going to have diarrhea. Brooke looked so ashamed, so humiliated, so sad. It was hard for us—me, Lilly, Ebony, and Manda—but it seemed like torture for Brooke. I think she came there thinking she was going to be the "outsider," and I think she thought we were going to gang up on her. But, Mrs. Seybolt is really cool. She has a way of keeping everything so organized—and so safe. She spoke first and told us how she'd like it to go. She said that only one person could talk at a time. We had to use "I" words, not "you" words. She said that this was not a persecution; it was more a cleansing. She said she hoped that we five girls could come up with a solution, a "treatment plan" that would allow all of us to, at the very least, "interact in a civil manner with each other." She said we didn't have to like each other or hang around together, "but when circumstances or activities require us to be in the same place," she hoped that "we could each be civil toward the other, and respect each other's feelings."

And then, Ivy, we each, one by one, had to talk to Brooke—to tell her in our "I" words how things she had said to us or done to us made us feel. I was the first to go, and I was really nervous, but Mrs. Seybolt reminded us that it was important to list those things so that it would be clear to Brooke what each one of us was upset about. We had to look at Brooke while we spoke, and she had to look at us.

So that's what I did. Once I started, it felt good to finally get it off my chest, to let it out, to know that Brooke would now know the things that had upset me. Mrs. Seybolt had to remind me a few times to use only the "I" words. This is what I said: "When I overheard you in the bathroom that day, Brooke, telling Manda and the other girls that I was a snot, that I thought I was better than everyone else because I came from a hoity-toity school in Cape Cod—well—I felt hurt because that is not what I think. I already felt nervous about starting at a new school and about making new friends, and when I heard you say that, I felt hurt and angry and afraid and disappointed that you felt like that about me, and I felt worried that the other girls would believe you and think that that was the kind of girl I was. And I felt sad."

It was weird, Ivy. Brooke listened to my every word and didn't try to interrupt once. And then, when it was her turn to speak, she started crying and said how sorry she was. She said that she really liked me and didn't know why she had said those things. And then Mrs. Seybolt said, "Brooke, I think maybe you do know why you said those things. Think about it for a minute. You said you like Olivia. What exactly are the things you like about Olivia?"

I almost died when I heard her answers, Ivy! She said I was pretty; that I had beautiful blond hair and blue eyes; that I was smart without showing off; that I had a nice way of listening to people when they spoke to me; that I seemed to make people relax around me; that I seemed able to talk to anyone, even grown-ups; that I was funny, kind, respectful, and nice to everyone; and that everyone seemed to like me as soon as they met me. Then she said that I was a fast runner, and she worried that I would soon be better than her.

Mrs. Seybolt asked Brooke if there were any of my qualities that she wished she herself had. And then Brooke looked very sad and sort of half laughed and said, "Yeah, all of them."

Then Mrs. Seybolt had Ebony do the same—and then Manda and, finally, Lilly. They all looked Brooke in the eye and told her how they felt about what she had done to hurt them. Then Brooke had to list what she liked about each one of them. And each time, when Mrs. Seybolt asked Brooke if there were any of their qualities that she wished she had, Brooke said the same thing: "All of them."

Then Mrs. Seybolt turned the tables on us, and we had to look at Brooke and tell her what we liked about her. I said how I loved her thick and curly sandy-brown hair and the way the gold flecks sparkled in her brown eyes. I said I appreciated how kind she was to me on the bus on my first day of school, and how she helped me to find my way around campus. I told her how touched I was that she thought to invite me to join her, Manda, and Lilly at her sleepover and how funny I thought she was during the truth-or-dare game. I told her how impressed I was with her running skills.

I remember how flabbergasted Brooke looked when I told her those things. And I remember how moved she was when she heard from the others about the things they liked about her. It was then that it became sadly clear to me that Brooke really had no idea that she had such nice qualities. I guess no one—not even her parents—ever made it clear to her that she was special.

And then we all talked—while Mrs. Seybolt listened—about how we might go forward. We all decided that maybe Brooke should be allowed to go back to school and back to school activities on a trial basis. We decided that we would all work on being real friends, because it had become clear to us—and to Brooke—that we really all did like each other. And Brooke admitted that she really wanted this, that she realized that we are the kind of friends that she wants and needs. Brooke thanked us for this chance and asked us to tell her right away if she starts to say or do things that upset us.

There was more to it than what I just wrote. But, Ivy, suddenly I am exhausted, and I think I will "hit the hay" as Daddy used to say. ☺

I miss you, Ivy! Kisses and hugs to you and Mommy and Daddy.

Love,
Livi (and Buffy too!) ☺

30

On Sunday I needed to unwind. It had been the week from hell and had really taken a toll on me. Our first official cross-country meet was coming up on Tuesday, so I decided to go for a run all by myself in the woods behind my house. Besides working on my times, I needed the solitude to quiet my mind.

It was the last week of October, and there was a winter feel to the air. The trees were almost bare, and their autumn leaves blanketed the ground and trails as far as I could see. The only sounds I heard were the songs of the birds above and the crunching of leaves under my feet. With every exhale I could see puffs of my breath before me. I really had to concentrate on my breathing. With all the meetings and drama of last week, I had missed two practices, and I felt a little off kilter.

I remembered what Miss Curtis had told me last week at one of the practices that I managed to get to. "Livi, I *know* you can go faster, but you are in training, and I want you to understand the sport. Proper training is more important than speed at this time. Running smart is more important than running fast. I want you to hold back—don't go out in front at the beginning of the race. You have a lot of potential Livi—I see a great future for you in running—so I don't want you to worry about the other girls in the race. Don't worry about what they are doing. You can't control what they do. You can only focus on yourself and control your own race."

As I ran, I tried to focus on the upcoming race against Rixtown Middle School, but my mind kept wandering. The turmoil and disruptions over the past few weeks had left me feeling terribly unsettled. But the longer I ran, and the deeper into the forest I went, the more my mind quieted and the more I felt at peace. I was hopeful that the recent confusion and upheaval would result in order and harmony.

Brooke had returned to school four days earlier, on Wednesday, and no one except for Ebony, Lilly, Manda, and I seemed to be aware that she had even been gone. It was very awkward at first. We knew it was unavoidable that our paths would cross. And they did—on Brooke's very first day back—in the cafeteria at lunch time.

Ebony and Lilly were already sitting together when I walked in. I scooted in next to Ebony and across from Lilly. Manda walked in, saw us, and hesitated. It was clear to me that she was uncertain if she should join us. Lilly made the first move by waving to her. I saw Manda almost melt with relief. When she sat down next to Lilly, she was trembling, and she looked everywhere but at us. Lilly looked across the table at us, wide-eyed and obviously not sure what to say or do. Then she turned toward Manda.

"Hey, Manda," she said quietly. "Glad you could join us."

"Oh my God, Lilly!" Manda said. A big tear dropped onto her lunch tray. She reached over and hugged Lilly. "I love you!" Then she looked across the table at Ebony and me. "I love you both too!" Another tear dropped onto her tray.

At the same time, Ebony and I leaned in and said, "We love you too!"

A moment later, I saw Brooke standing on the far side of the cafeteria. She stood alone and carried only a carton of milk. She was pale. She looked timid—almost frail—as she twirled a lock of hair around her finger. She scanned the room, and when our eyes met, she seemed to freeze. I felt my stomach flip-flop. I was shaking inside, but I knew what I had to do. I had already told Ebony and Lilly what I wanted to do—but I told them I would only do it if they both were okay with it. Ebony agreed it was time to bury the hatchet, time to move forward. Lilly admitted she was somewhat nervous about it, but said she was willing to do it because "it was the right thing to do."

So I waved at Brooke and motioned to her to join us. I saw her hesitate, take a deep breath, and then slowly walk across the cafeteria to our table. Her head was down, and she clutched the carton of milk with both hands.

"Hi," Brooke gulped, and looked only at me.

"Have a seat," I said as I slid down the bench toward Ebony. "Is that all you are eating?"

Brooke fumbled with the carton of milk. "Yeah. I'm not very hungry."

I looked across the table at Manda and Lilly, who looked shell-shocked. Lilly looked at me, gave me a half smile, and then looked toward Brooke.

"Are you going to practice after school today?" Lilly asked. Her voice shook. "We only have four more practices scheduled. And then—*gulp!*—our first meet is next Tuesday."

"I'm planning on it," Brooke said quietly. "I missed a whole lot of practices—as you know—so I am really out of shape." She took a deep breath and exhaled slowly. With eyes still downcast, she said, "Thanks, everyone, for letting me sit with you...I never expected..." Her voice trailed off.

Lilly leaned in across the table. "Look, Brooke," she said quietly, "we've all been through a rough time. Friends go through rough patches sometimes. That's life. But, hopefully our friendships will be better and stronger from now on. We all just have to keep it real and honest. If something is bothering any one of us, that person has to speak up and say what is bothering her. So none of us will ever have to wonder where we stand. That's what we agreed to do in Mrs. Seybolt's office. That's the plan. That's the only way this whole mess is going to get better—real and honest." Lilly looked around at all of us. "Right?"

Manda spoke next. "I think we should make a pinkie agreement. And I think we shouldn't bring this whole mess up again. It seems that we have said all there is to say on it. I think we have talked this thing to death!" She looked around the table, held her pinkie finger up in the air, and said, "Is everyone cool with making a pinkie agreement? And with burying this whole mess? And with never bringing it up again? And with keeping it real and honest?"

I smiled as I extended my arm and raised my pinkie finger toward the middle of the table. "I'm cool with that."

Ebony followed. With her pinkie finger raised, she said, "Me too. I'm cool with that."

"Yes, sir," Lilly said, saluting first and then raising her pinkie finger in an official gesture. "I am cool with that, sir!"

"Here, here!" Brooke said, and gulped again. A big tear spilled onto the table. "I am cool with that, sir!"

We five hooked our pinkie fingers together, tugged them firmly, and, as though we had rehearsed the ceremony, we shouted all together, "We are *cool* with that, sir!"

Laughing in sheer joy, we all fell back onto our benches. Those sitting at the tables near us—unaware of what we were pinkie-agreeing to—clapped and yelled in unison, "We are *cool* with that, sir!"

Before we knew it, the rest of the kids in the cafeteria joined in. "We are *cool* with that, sir!"

Even the cafeteria staff and the several teachers who were supervising our lunch period laughed, shrugged, and joined in. "We are *cool* with that, sir!"

Later that evening, just before I turned off my lamp, I jotted down a quick note in my diary.

Wednesday, October 23

Dear Ivy,
    What a day! All is well. And all I have to say is this: I am *cool* with that, sir! ☺

Love,
Livi

31

"On your mark...get set...*go!*"

I heard my own voice let out a throaty "*harumpf*" as I shot forward from my mark. Within seconds—and with almost no effort at all—I passed several runners: some were wearing Chelsea Middle School colors of red and white, like me, and some were wearing Rixtown Middle School's blue and gold.

The sky was gray, and the air was cold and damp. The two-mile Slater Trail was dotted on either side by eager fans and onlookers. I was familiar with this trail that wound its way through the woods at the edge of our Chelsea Middle School campus. Several small inclines made the route somewhat challenging, but my focus was on my breathing and my speed. I wanted to bolt out of the pack—I knew I could move out to the front runners—but I forced myself to hold back and concentrate on running a smart race rather than a fast race. Miss Curtis had really drummed that into me: "Remember, Livi... you are in training...understanding the sport and proper training are more important than the speed right now...running a smart race is more important than running a fast race. Don't worry about the other girls...you can't control what they do... you can only focus on yourself and control your own race."

So I held back. I concentrated on my own race. I looked straight ahead. And I still found myself passing slower runners.

My breathing was easy and steady, and my strides were long, powerful, and efficient.

I felt exuberant, alive, and full of joy. I felt Ivy running with me. Had it really only been three and a half months since Ivy, Mom, and Dad were killed in that horrendous car accident? Since they were ripped from my life? Since I was left to live in this world alone? I felt the sadness, despair, confusion, and fear of those past 110 days drain from my body. With each stride I took, I felt the heaviness and iciness around my heart thaw and melt away. I felt fresh and new. Not only was I focused on the race, but I was focused on my life, on my present, and on my future. The past was over and gone.

My strides became longer and easier. I whizzed by blurs of red, white, blue, and gold; the finish line was in sight. I heard the cheers of the fans and of the girls who already had crossed the finish line. I heard the encouraging shouts of Miss Curtis and Miss Jaynes. I heard *"Li-vi! Li-vi! Li-vi!"*

I caught a brief glimpse of Bobby Hendry standing near the finish line. He flashed me his beautiful smile as he gave me a thumbs-up. I saw Ivy waiting for me just beyond the finish line, arms folded across her chest, smiling from ear to ear. *I knew you could do it, Livs!* And right next to Ivy—jumping up and down, cheering me on, were Ebony, Brooke, and Lilly. Manda danced up and down from the sidelines, arms in the air, hands raised to the heavens. Chelsea Middle School had won the meet against Rixtown.

I fell into the arms of my four best friends. We had done it. Out of 120 girls, Ebony, Brooke, Lilly, and I had placed in the top twenty. And Manda couldn't have been prouder or happier for us all.

Our celebration went on for a while, even when a sudden downpour soaked us to the bone. We danced in the rain, and we welcomed all the compliments and the pats on our backs.

We knew we deserved all that. We each had worked hard, and we each had done our best. We had many more schools to face, many more races to run, and many more challenges to conquer—and we looked forward to that. We felt ready.

But over and above all that, we each had accomplished a whole lot more than running a good race. We had overcome a mountain of some pretty serious obstacles. We had learned some pretty intense lessons of life. Together we had looked at all sides of bullying, stared it in the eyes, and decided it was not acceptable in any shape or form. But we went further than that. We went inside of bullying and felt how it affected each one of us, and we decided we wanted to learn how to live with each other in a way that let us each feel respected and safe, feel free to feel every emotion, and feel free to learn and grow from every experience that life would give us.

We chose to keep our friendships real and honest—and to help each other out along the way. Because that is what friends do.

We chose to follow our hearts, to share our truths, and to dance in the rain.

32

It was the day after our first victory, and I was feeling pretty proud of myself. Unable to concentrate on my homework, I tossed my book aside and got up from my bed. I plopped down onto my rocking chair and stared up at the painting. I was still in awe of the remarkable image that I had painted—the incredible likeness of my total and complete memory of my time spent with Ivy. I was still trying to convince myself that my experience had been real. My mind-set kept flip-flopping. One minute I believed, with no doubt, that my memory was of a real event—that I really had somehow crossed over to an unknown world and had shared a few moments in time with my beloved Ivy. And then, one moment later, I believed that it must have all been a dream, because experiences like that just don't happen in real life. But as I stared up at my painting, I knew that there was no way that I could have ever been able to produce a work of art—a wonderful creation like *The Visit*—had I not really experienced it firsthand.

The messages I had received over the past three and a half months from Ivy seemed so real. The nearness of Ivy and her words of wisdom had inspired me to go on when I felt I wouldn't make it. Ivy's communications to me—real or not—had kept me from giving up and had helped me to somehow move forward.

I slowly rocked in my chair—back and forth, back and forth—as I continued to study my painting. I shivered as I remembered all that I had experienced—or thought I had experienced—on that day. If only Ivy would give me a sign—any sign—that would prove it was all real.

The old rocker creaked as I slowly got up and walked over to my dresser. I opened the drawer, reached to the back, and slid open the secret compartment. Maybe if I wrote to Ivy and explained how confused I felt, if I told her how badly I needed some sign to let me know if her visit had been real or just a very vivid dream, maybe she would somehow give me the answer I was looking for. I fumbled for my diary, pulled it out, and clutched it to my chest. I sighed as I slowly sat down onto my bed. I gently moved my hand across the book's soft quilted cover and traced the red, pink, and yellow tulips with my fingertip. I carefully untied the red ribbons and opened my diary. Once again, I was overwhelmed with the aroma of Mom's Jontue—or was it Grammie's? I still had not ever smelled Jontue when I hugged Grammie. When I had asked her once if she had ever used the same perfume that Mom had used, Grammie had smiled and said, "I don't think so. I've been using Eternity for... well...an eternity." She had laughed. "I really don't know why you smell Jontue when you open the journal," she said. "It's been sitting in my vanity drawer for many years, Olivia—ever since your mom gave it to me when she was just about your age."

I guessed I would never solve that mystery. I only knew that each time I opened my journal, I felt close to Mom. And for that, I was thankful.

I spotted my note dated Wednesday, October 23—and smiled when I read what I had written: "*I am* cool *with that, sir!* ☺" I was certain that Ivy must have gotten a kick out of *that*. Still smiling, I sighed a long happy sigh. I quickly scanned my next letter that was dated October 26, and then turned to the first blank page so that I could write to Ivy.

What I saw took my breath away! I was stunned. A jolt of electricity ran down my spine and all the way to my toes. The hair on the back of my neck stood up, and my arms bristled with goose bumps. I stared in disbelief.

"What?!" I said out loud. An unfamiliar printed chicken scratch was scrawled in ink across the page. It looked like a foreign language. I was confused. *Who wrote this? Why would someone write in my diary?* The longer I stared at the scribble, the more it seemed oddly familiar to me—even though I still couldn't read what it said. The letters were all jumbled together—and backward!

"What?!" I said out loud again. "What in the world is going on here?"

And then I got an idea. I bolted up from my bed and ran over to my dresser. I held the message up to my mirror. It took me a few seconds to focus my eyes, but slowly, I began to read the message. The printed chicken scratch suddenly looked very familiar to me.

> Dear Livi,
> You need to know that our visit was as real to me as it was to you. We were blessed with that special moment in time. Don't question it. Believe. And always follow your heart. Share your truths. Dance in the rain. Every day I am alive in your sunshine as you are alive in mine.
> Luv Y

I stared at Ivy's message for a long time. I read it over and over and over. There was no longer any doubt in my mind. My visit to Ivy's world had been real, just as her visits to my world had really happened. Knowing that—*really knowing that*—filled me with a peace I had not known was possible. Ivy's handwritten message to me on that Wednesday, October 30, gave me all the answers I had been looking for. I felt joy in my heart, and I knew I would be okay as I made my way through life.

Clutching my diary to my heart, I settled into my rocking chair. The late October sun suddenly burst through a cloud and sent radiated shafts of sunlight through my two windows. The sunbeams seemed to settle directly on me as I rocked back and forth, and they warmed my body and my soul. Ivy's message said that she was alive in my sunshine, each and every day, just as I was alive in hers. I knew I was not alone—it would always be me, myself, and Ivy—and I was certain that someday we would be together again. But, until then, I knew I had so much living to do. So much living to do.

Made in the USA
Middletown, DE
06 June 2015